Chronicles of Martin Hewitt by Arthur Morrison

Arthur Morrison was born on November 1st, 1863, in Poplar, in the East End of London. From the age of 8, after the death of his father, he was brought up, along with two siblings, by his mother, Jane.

Morrison spent his youth in the East End. In 1879 he began as an office boy in the Architect's Department of the London School Board and, in his spare time, visited used bookstores in Whitechapel Road. He first published, a humorous poem, in the magazine Cycling in 1880.

In 1885 Morrison began writing for The Globe newspaper. In 1886, he switched to the People's Palace, in Mile End and, in 1888, published the Cockney Corner collection, about life in Soho, Whitechapel, Bow Street and other areas of London.

By 1889 he was an editor at the Palace Journal, reprinting some earlier sketches, and writing commentaries on books and articles on the life of the London poor.

By 1890 he was back at The Globe and published 'The Shadows Around Us', a supernatural collection of stories. Also at this time he began to develop a keen interest in Japanese Art.

In October 1891 his short story A Street appeared in Macmillan's Magazine. The following year he married Elizabeth Thatcher and then befriended publisher and poet William Ernest Henley for whom he wrote stories of working-class life in Henley's National Observer between 1892-94.

In 1894 came his first detective story featuring Martin Hewitt, described as "a low-key, realistic, lower-class answer to Sherlock Holmes".

Morrison published A Child of the Jago in 1896 swiftly followed by The Adventures of Martin Hewitt.

In 1897 Morrison wrote seven stories about Horace Dorrington, a deeply corrupt private detective, described as "a cheerfully unrepentant sociopath who is willing to stoop to theft, blackmail, fraud or cold-blooded murder to make a dishonest penny."

To London Town, the final part of a trilogy including Tales of Mean Streets and A Child of the Jago was published in 1899. Following on came a wide spectrum of works, including novels, short stories and one act plays.

In 1911 he published his authoritative work Japanese Painters, illustrated with art from his own collection.

Although he retired from journalistic work in 1913 he continued to write about Art.

In his last decades Morrison served as a special constable, and reported on the first Zeppelin raid on London. Tragically in 1921 his son, Guy, who had survived the war, died of malaria.

The Royal Society of Literature elected him as a member in 1924 and to its Council in 1935.

In 1930 he moved to Chalfont St Peter, Buckinghamshire. Here he wrote the short story collection Fiddle o' Dreams and More.

Index of Contents

I. — THE IVY COTTAGE MYSTERY

I had been working double tides for a month: at night on my morning paper, as usual; and in the morning on an evening paper as locum tenens for another man who was taking a holiday. This was an exhausting plan of work, although it only actually involved some six hours' attendance a day, or less, at the two offices. I turned up at the headquarters of my own paper at ten in the evening, and by the time I had seen the editor, selected a subject, written my leader, corrected the slips, chatted, smoked, and so on, and cleared off, it was very usually one o'clock. This meant bed at two, or even three, after supper at the club.

This was all very well at ordinary periods, when any time in the morning would do for rising, but when I had to be up again soon after seven, and round at the evening paper office by eight, I naturally felt a little worn and disgusted with things by midday, after a sharp couple of hours' leaderette scribbling and paragraphing, with attendant sundries.

But the strain was over, and on the first day of comparative comfort I indulged in a midday breakfast and the first undisgusted glance at a morning paper for a month. I felt rather interested in an inquest, begun the day before, on the body of a man whom I had known very slightly before I took to living in chambers.

His name was Gavin Kingscote, and he was an artist of a casual and desultory sort, having, I believe, some small private means of his own. As a matter of fact, he had boarded in the same house in which I had lodged myself for a while, but as I was at the time a late homer and a fairly early riser, taking no regular board in the house, we never became much acquainted. He had since, I understood, made some judicious Stock Exchange speculations, and had set up house in Finchley.

Now the news was that he had been found one morning murdered in his smoking-room, while the room itself, with others, was in a state of confusion. His pockets had been rifled, and his watch and chain were gone, with one or two other small articles of value. On the night of the tragedy a friend had sat smoking with him in the room where the murder took place, and he had been the last person to see Mr Kingscote alive. A jobbing gardener, who kept the garden in order by casual work from time to time, had been arrested in consequence of footprints, exactly corresponding with his boots, having been found on the garden beds near the French window of the smoking-room.

I finished my breakfast and my paper, and Mrs Clayton, the housekeeper, came to clear my table. She was sister of my late landlady of the house where Kingscote had lodged, and it was by this connection that I had found my chambers. I had not seen the housekeeper since the crime was first reported, so I now said:

"This is shocking news of Mr Kingscote, Mrs Clayton. Did you know him yourself?"

She had apparently only been waiting for some such remark to burst out with whatever information she possessed.

"Yes, sir," she exclaimed: "shocking indeed. Pore young feller! I see him often when I was at my sister's, and he was always a nice, quiet gentleman, so different from some. My sister, she's awful cut up, sir, I assure you. And what d'you think 'appened, sir, only last Tuesday? You remember Mr Kingscote's room where he painted the woodwork so beautiful with gold flowers, and blue, and pink? He used to tell my sister she'd always have something to remember him by. Well, two young fellers, gentlemen I can't call them, come and took that room (it being to let), and went and scratched off all the paint in mere wicked mischief, and then chopped up all the panels into sticks and bits! Nice sort o' gentlemen them! And then they bolted in the morning, being afraid, I s'pose, of being made to pay after treating a pore widder's property like that. That was only Tuesday, and the very next day the pore young gentleman himself's dead, murdered in his own 'ouse, and him goin' to be married an' all! Dear, dear! I remember once he said—"

Mrs Clayton was a good soul, but once she began to talk some one else had to stop her. I let her run on for a reasonable time, and then rose and prepared to go out. I remembered very well the panels that had been so mischievously destroyed. They made the room the showroom of the house, which was an old one. They were indeed less than half finished when I came away, and Mrs Lamb, the landlady, had shown them to me one day when Kingscote was out. All the walls of the room were panelled and painted white, and Kingscote had put upon them an eccentric but charming decoration, obviously suggested by some of the work of Mr Whistler. Tendrils, flowers, and butterflies in a quaint convention wandered thinly from panel to panel, giving the otherwise rather uninteresting room an unwonted atmosphere of richness and elegance. The lamentable jackasses who had destroyed this had certainly selected the best feature of the room whereon to inflict their senseless mischief.

I strolled idly downstairs, with no particular plan for the afternoon in my mind, and looked in at Hewitt's offices. Hewitt was reading a note, and after a little chat he informed me that it had been left an hour ago, in his absence, by the brother of the man I had just been speaking of.

"He isn't quite satisfied," Hewitt said, "with the way the police are investigating the case, and asks me to run down to Finchley and look round. Yesterday I should have refused, because I have five cases in progress already, but today I find that circumstances have given me a day or two. Didn't you say you knew the man?"

"Scarcely more than by sight. He was a boarder in the house at Chelsea where I stayed before I started chambers."

"Ah, well; I think I shall look into the thing. Do you feel particularly interested in the case? I mean, if you've nothing better to do, would you come with me?"

"I shall be very glad," I said. "I was in some doubt what to do with myself. Shall you start at once?"

"I think so. Kerrett, just call a cab. By the way, Brett, which paper has the fullest report of the inquest yesterday? I'll run over it as we go down."

As I had only seen one paper that morning, I could not answer Hewitt's question. So we bought various papers as we went along in the cab, and I found the reports while Martin Hewitt studied them. Summarized, this was the evidence given:

Sarah Dodson, general servant, deposed that she had been in service at Ivy Cottage, the residence of the deceased, for five months, the only other regular servant being the housekeeper and cook. On the evening of the previous Tuesday both servants retired a little before eleven, leaving Mr Kingscote with a friend in the smoking or sitting room. She never saw her master again alive. On coining downstairs the following morning and going to open the smoking-room windows, she was horrified to discover the body of Mr Kingscote lying on the floor of the room with blood about the head. She at once raised an alarm, and, on the instructions of the housekeeper, fetched a doctor, and gave information to the police. In answer to questions, witness stated she had heard no noise of any sort during the night, nor had anything suspicious occurred.

Hannah Carr, housekeeper and cook, deposed that she had been in the late Mr Kingscote's service since he had first taken Ivy Cottage—a period of rather more than a year. She had last seen the deceased alive on the evening of the previous Tuesday, at half-past ten, when she knocked at the door of the smoking-room, where Mr Kingscote was sitting with a friend, to ask if he would require anything more. Nothing was required, so witness shortly after went to bed. In the morning she was called by the previous witness, who had just gone downstairs, and found the body of deceased lying as described. Deceased's watch and chain were gone, as also was a ring he usually wore, and his pockets appeared to have been turned out. All the ground floor of the house was in confusion, and a bureau, a writing-table, and various drawers were open—a bunch of keys usually carried by deceased being left hanging at one keyhole. Deceased had drawn some money from the bank on the Tuesday, for current expenses; how much she did not know. She had not heard or seen anything suspicious during the night. Besides Dodson and herself, there were no regular servants; there was a charwoman, who came occasionally, and a jobbing gardener, living near, who was called in as required.

Mr James Vidler, surgeon, had been called by the first witness between seven and eight on Wednesday morning. He found the deceased lying on his face on the floor of the smoking-room, his feet being about eighteen inches from the window, and his head lying in the direction of the fireplace. He found three large contused wounds on the head, any one of which would probably have caused death. The wounds had all been inflicted, apparently, with the same blunt instrument—probably a club or life preserver, or other similar weapon. They could not have been done with the poker. Death was due to concussion of the brain, and deceased had probably been dead seven or eight hours when witness saw him. He had since examined the body more closely, but found no marks at all indicative of a struggle having taken place; indeed, from the position of the wounds and their severity, he should judge that the deceased had been attacked unawares from behind, and had died at once. The body appeared to be perfectly healthy.

Then there was police evidence, which showed that all the doors and windows were found shut and completely fastened, except the front door, which, although shut, was not bolted. There were shutters behind the French windows in the smoking-room, and these were found fastened. No money was found in the bureau, nor in any of the opened drawers, so that if any had been there, it had been stolen. The pockets were entirely empty, except for a small pair of nail scissors, and there was no watch upon the body, nor a ring. Certain footprints were found on the garden beds, which had led the police to take certain steps. No footprints were to be seen on the garden path, which was hard gravel.

Mr Alexander Campbell, stockbroker, stated that he had known deceased for some few years, and had done business for him. He and Mr Kingscote frequently called on one another, and on Tuesday evening they dined together at Ivy Cottage. They sat smoking and chatting till nearly twelve o'clock, when Mr Kingscote himself let him out, the servants having gone to bed. Here the witness proceeded rather excitedly: "That is all I know of this horrible business, and I can say nothing else. What the police mean by following and watching me—"

The Coroner: "Pray be calm, Mr Campbell. The police must do what seems best to them in a case of this sort. I am sure you would not have them neglect any means of getting at the truth."

Witness: "Certainly not. But if they suspect me, why don't they say so? It is intolerable that I should be—"

The Coroner: "Order, order, Mr Campbell. You are here to give evidence."

The witness then, in answer to questions, stated that the French windows of the smoking-room had been left open during the evening, the weather being very warm. He could not recollect whether or not deceased closed them before he left, but he certainly did not close the shutters. Witness saw nobody near the house when he left.

Mr Douglas Kingscote, architect, said deceased was his brother. He had not seen him for some months, living as he did in another part of the country. He believed his brother was fairly well off, and he knew that he had made a good amount by speculation in the last year or two. Knew of no person who would be likely to owe his brother a grudge, and could suggest no motive for the crime except ordinary robbery. His brother was to have been married in a few weeks. Questioned further on this point, witness said that the marriage was to have taken place a year ago, and it was with that view that Ivy Cottage, deceased's residence, was taken. The lady, however, sustained a domestic bereavement, and afterwards went abroad with her family: she was, witness believed, shortly expected back to England.

William Bates, jobbing gardener, who was brought up in custody, was cautioned, but elected to give evidence. Witness, who appeared to be much agitated, admitted having been in the garden of Ivy Cottage at four in the morning, but said that he had only gone to attend to certain plants, and knew absolutely nothing of the murder. He however admitted that he had no order for work beyond what he had done the day before. Being further pressed, witness made various contradictory statements, and finally said that he had gone to take certain plants away.

The inquest was then adjourned.

This was the cast as it stood—apparently not a case presenting any very striking feature, although there seemed to me to be doubtful peculiarities in many parts of it. I asked Hewitt what he thought.

"Quite impossible to think anything, my boy, just yet; wait till we see the place. There are any number of possibilities. Kingscote's friend, Campbell, may have come in again, you know, by way of the window—or he may not. Campbell may have owed him money or something—or he may not. The anticipated wedding may have something to do with it—or, again, that may not. There is no limit to the possibilities, as far as we see from this report—a mere dry husk of the affair. When we get closer we shall examine the possibilities by the light of more detailed information. One probability is that the wretched gardener is innocent. It seems to me that his was only a comparatively blameless manoeuvre not unheard of at other times in his trade. He came at four in the morning to steal away the flowers he had planted the day before, and felt rather bashful when questioned on the point. Why should he trample on the beds, else? I wonder if the police thought to examine the beds for traces of rooting up, or questioned the housekeeper as to any plants being missing? But we shall see."

We chatted at random as the train drew near Finchley, and I mentioned inter alia the wanton piece of destruction perpetrated at Kingscote's late lodgings. Hewitt was interested.

"That was curious," he said, "very curious. Was anything else damaged? Furniture and so forth?"

"I don't know. Mrs Clayton said nothing of it, and I didn't ask her. But it was quite bad enough as it was. The decoration was really good, and I can't conceive a meaner piece of tomfoolery than such an attack on a decent woman's property."

Then Hewitt talked of other cases of similar stupid damage by creatures inspired by a defective sense of humour, or mere love of mischief. He had several curious and sometimes funny anecdotes of such affairs at museums and picture exhibitions, where the damage had been so great as to induce the authorities to call him in to discover the offender. The work was not always easy, chiefly from the mere absence of intelligible motive; not, indeed, always successful. One of the anecdotes related to a case of malicious damage to a picture—the outcome of blind artistic jealousy—a case which had been hushed up by a large expenditure in compensation. It would considerably startle most people, could it be printed here, with the actual names of the parties concerned.

Ivy Cottage, Finchley, was a compact little house, standing in a compact little square of garden, little more than a third of an acre, or perhaps no more at all. The front door was but a dozen yards or so back from the road, but the intervening space was well treed and shrubbed. Mr Douglas Kingscote had not yet returned from town, but the housekeeper, an intelligent, matronly woman, who knew of his intention to call in Martin Hewitt, was ready to show us the house.

"First," Hewitt said, when we stood in the smoking-room, "I observe that somebody has shut the drawers and the bureau. That is unfortunate. Also, the floor has been washed and the carpet taken up, which is much worse. That, I suppose, was because the police had finished their examination, but it doesn't help me to make one at all. Has anything—anything at all—been left as it was on Tuesday morning?"

"Well, sir, you see everything was in such a muddle," the housekeeper began, "and when the police had done—"

"Just so. I know. You 'set it to rights', eh? Oh, that setting to rights! It has lost me a fortune at one time and another. As to the other rooms, now, have they been set to rights?"

"Such as was disturbed have been put right, sir, of course."

"Which were disturbed? Let me see them. But wait a moment."

He opened the French windows, and closely examined the catch and bolts. He knelt and inspected the holes whereinto the bolts fell, and then glanced casually at the folding shutters. He opened a drawer or two, and tried the working of the locks with the keys the housekeeper carried. They were, the housekeeper explained, Mr Kingscote's own keys. All through the lower floors Hewitt examined some things attentively and closely, and others with scarcely a glance, on a system unaccountable to me. Presently, he asked to be shown Mr Kingscote's bedroom, which had not been disturbed, "set to rights," or slept in since the crime. Here, the housekeeper said, all drawers were kept unlocked but two—one in the wardrobe and one in the dressing-table, which Mr Kingscote had always been careful to keep locked. Hewitt immediately pulled both drawers open without difficulty. Within, in addition to a few odds and ends, were papers. All the contents of these drawers had been turned over confusedly, while those of the unlocked drawers were in perfect order.

"The police," Hewitt remarked, "may not have observed these matters. Any more than such an ordinary thing as this," he added, picking up a bent nail lying at the edge of a rug.

The housekeeper doubtless took the remark as a reference to the entire unimportance of a bent nail, but I noticed that Hewitt dropped the article quietly into his pocket.

We came away. At the front gate we met Mr Douglas Kingscote, who had just returned from town. He introduced himself, and expressed surprise at our promptitude both of coming and going.

"You can't have got anything like a clue in this short time, Mr Hewitt?" he asked.

"Well, no," Hewitt replied, with a certain dryness, "perhaps not. But I doubt whether a month's visit would have helped me to get anything very striking out of a washed floor and a houseful of carefully cleaned-up and 'set-to-rights' rooms. Candidly, I don't think you can reasonably expect much of me. The police have a much better chance—they had the scene of the crime to examine. I have seen just such a few rooms as anyone might see in the first well-furnished house he might enter. The trail of the housemaid has overlaid all the others."

"I'm very sorry for that; the fact was, I expected rather more of the police; and, indeed, I wasn't here in time entirely to prevent the clearing up. But still, I thought your well-known powers—"

"My dear sir, my 'well-known powers' are nothing but common sense assiduously applied and made quick by habit. That won't enable me to see the invisible."

"But can't we have the rooms put back into something of the state they were in? The cook will remember—"

"No, no. That would be worse and worse: that would only be the housemaid's trail in turn overlaid by the cook's. You must leave things with me for a little, I think."

"Then you don't give the case up?" Mr Kingscote asked anxiously.

"Oh, no! I don't give it up just yet. Do you know anything of your brother's private papers—as they were before his death?"

"I never knew anything till after that. I have gone over them, but they are all very ordinary letters. Do you suspect a theft of papers?"

Martin Hewitt, with his hands on his stick behind him, looked sharply at the other, and shook his head. "No," he said, "I can't quite say that."

We bade Mr Douglas Kingscote good-day, and walked towards the station. "Great nuisance, that setting to rights," Hewitt observed, on the way. "If the place had been left alone, the job might have been settled one way or another by this time. As it is, we shall have to run over to your old lodgings."

"My old lodgings?" I repeated, amazed. "Why my old lodgings?"

Hewitt turned to me with a chuckle and a wide smile. "Because we can't see the broken panel-work anywhere else," he said. "Let's see—Chelsea, isn't it?"

"Yes, Chelsea. But why—you don't suppose the people who defaced the panels also murdered the man who painted them?"

"Well," Hewitt replied, with another smile, "that would be carrying a practical joke rather far, wouldn't it? Even for the ordinary picture damager."

"You mean you don't think they did it, then? But what do you mean?"

"My dear fellow, I don't mean anything but what I say. Come now, this is rather an interesting case despite appearances, and it has interested me: so much, in fact, that I really think I forgot to offer Mr Douglas Kingscote my condolence on his bereavement. You see a problem is a problem, whether of theft, assassination, intrigue, or anything else, and I only think of it as one. The work very often makes me forget merely human sympathies. Now, you have often been good enough to express a very flattering interest in my work, and you shall have an opportunity of exercising your own common sense in the way I am always having to exercise mine. You shall see all my evidence (if I'm lucky enough to get any) as I collect it, and you shall make your own inferences. That will be a little exercise for you; the sort of exercise I should give a pupil if I had one. But I will give you what information I have, and you shall start fairly from this moment. You know the inquest evidence such as it was, and you saw everything I did in Ivy Cottage?"

"Yes; I think so. But I'm not much the wiser."

"Very well. Now I will tell you. What does the whole case look like? How would you class the crime?"

"I suppose as the police do. An ordinary case of murder with the object of robbery."

"It is not an ordinary case. If it were, I shouldn't know as much as I do, little as that is; the ordinary cases are always difficult. The assailant did not come to commit a burglary, although he was a skilled burglar, or one of them was, if more than one were concerned. The affair has, I think, nothing to do with the expected wedding, nor had Mr Campbell anything to do in it—at any rate, personally—nor the gardener. The criminal (or one of them) was known personally to the dead man, and was well-dressed: he (or again one of them, and I think there were two) even had a chat with Mr Kingscote before the murder took place. He came to ask for something which Mr Kingscote was unwilling to part with,—perhaps hadn't got. It was not a bulky thing. Now you have all my materials before you."

"But all this doesn't look like the result of the blind spite that would ruin a man's work first and attack him bodily afterwards."

"Spite isn't always blind, and there are other blind things besides spite; people with good eyes in their heads are blind sometimes, even detectives."

"But where did you get all this information? What makes you suppose that this was a burglar who didn't want to burgle, and a well-dressed man, and so on?"

Hewitt chuckled and smiled again.

"I saw it—saw it, my boy, that's all," he said "But here comes the train."

On the way back to town, after I had rather minutely described Kingscote's work on the boarding-house panels, Hewitt asked me for the names and professions of such fellow lodgers in that house as I might remember. "When did you leave yourself?" he ended.

"Three years ago, or rather more. I can remember Kingscote himself; Turner, a medical student—James Turner, I think; Harvey Challitt, diamond merchant's articled pupil—he was a bad egg entirely, he's doing five years for forgery now; by the bye he had the room we are going to see till he was marched off, and Kingscote took it—a year before I left; there was Norton—don't know what he was 'something in the City', I think; and Carter Paget, in the Admiralty Office. I don't remember any more at this moment; there were pretty frequent changes. But you can get it all from Mrs Lamb, of course."

"Of course; and Mrs Lamb's exact address is—what?"

I gave him the address, and the conversation became disjointed. At Farringdon station, where we alighted, Hewitt called two hansoms. Preparing to enter one, he motioned me to the other, saying, "You get straight away to Mrs Lamb's at once. She may be going to burn that splintered wood, or to set things to rights, after the manner of her kind, and you can stop her. I must make one or two small inquiries, but I shall be there half an hour after you."

"Shall I tell her our object?"

"Only that I may be able to catch her mischievous lodgers—nothing else yet." He jumped into the hansom and was gone.

I found Mrs Lamb still in a state of indignant perturbation over the trick served her four days before. Fortunately, she had left everything in the panelled room exactly as she had found it, with an idea of being better able to demand or enforce reparation should her lodgers return. "The room's theirs, you see, sir," she said, "till the end of the week, since they paid in advance, and they may come back and offer to make amends, although I doubt it. As pleasant-spoken a young chap as you might wish, he seemed, him as come to take the rooms. 'My cousin,' says he, 'is rather an invalid, havin' only just got over congestion of the lungs, and he won't be in London till this evening late. He's comin' up from Birmingham,' he ses, 'and I hope he won't catch a fresh cold on the way, although of course we've got him muffled up plenty.' He took the rooms, sir, like a gentleman, and mentioned several gentlemen's names I knew well, as had lodged here before; and then he put down on that there very table, sir"—Mrs Lamb indicated the exact spot with her hand, as though that made the whole thing much more wonderful—"he put down on that very table a week's rent in advance, and ses, 'That's always the best sort of reference, Mrs Lamb, I think,' as kind-mannered as anything—and never 'aggled about the amount nor nothing. He only had a little black bag, but he said his cousin had all the luggage coming in the train, and as there was so much, p'r'aps they wouldn't get it here till next day. Then he went out and came in with his cousin at eleven that night—Sarah let 'em in her own self—and in the morning they was gone—and this!" Poor Mrs Lamb, plaintively indignant, stretched her arm towards the wrecked panels.

"If the gentleman as you say is comin' on, sir," she pursued, "can do anything to find 'em, I'll prosecute 'em, that I will, if it costs me ten pound. I spoke to the constable on the beat, but he only looked like a fool, and said if I knew where they were I might charge 'em with wilful damage, or county court 'em. Of course I know I can do that if I knew where they were, but how can I find 'em? Mr Jones he said his name was; but how many Joneses is there in London, sir?"

I couldn't imagine any answer to a question like this, but I condoled with Mrs Lamb as well as I could. She afterwards went on to express herself much as her sister had done with regard to Kingscote's death, only as the destruction of her panels loomed larger in her mind, she dwelt primarily on that. "It might almost seem," she said, "that somebody had a deadly spite on the pore young gentleman, and went breakin' up his paintin' one night, and murderin' him the next!"

I examined the broken panels with some care, having half a notion to attempt to deduce something from them myself, if possible. But I could deduce nothing. The beading had been taken out, and the panels, which were thick in the centre but bevelled at the edges, had been removed and split up literally into thin firewood, which lay in a tumbled heap on the hearth and about the floor. Every panel in the room had been treated in the same way, and the result was a pretty large heap of sticks, with nothing whatever about them to distinguish them from other sticks, except the paint on one face, which I observed in many places had been scratched and scraped away. The rug was drawn half across the hearth, and had evidently been used to deaden the sound of chopping. But mischief—wanton and stupid mischief—was all I could deduce from it all.

Mr Jones's cousin, it seemed, only Sarah had seen, as she admitted him in the evening, and then he was so heavily muffled that she could not distinguish his features, and would never be able to identify him. But as for the other one, Mrs Lamb was ready to swear to him anywhere.

Hewitt was long in coming, and internal symptoms of the approach of dinner-time (we had had no lunch) had made themselves felt before a sharp ring at the door-bell foretold his arrival. "I have had to wait for answers to a telegram," he said in explanation, "but at any rate I have the information I wanted. And these are the mysterious panels, are they?"

Mrs Lamb's true opinion of Martin Hewitt's behaviour as it proceeded would have been amusing to know. She watched in amazement the antics of a man who purposed finding out who had been splitting sticks by dint of picking up each separate stick and staring at it. In the end he collected a small handful of sticks by themselves and handed them to me, saying. "Just put these together on the table, Brett, and see what you make of them."

I turned the pieces painted side up, and fitted them together into a complete panel, joining up the painted design accurately. "It is an entire panel," I said.

"Good. Now look at the sticks a little more closely, and tell me if you notice anything peculiar about them—any particular in which they? differ from all the others."

I looked. "Two adjoining sticks," I said, "have each a small semi-circular cavity stuffed with what seems to be putty. Put together it would mean a small circular hole, perhaps a knot-hole, half an inch or so in diameter, in the panel, filled in with putty, or whatever it is."

"A knot-hole?" Hewitt asked, with particular emphasis.

"Well, no, not a knot-hole, of course, because that would go right through, and this doesn't. It is probably less than half an inch deep from the front surface."

"Anything else? Look at the whole appearance of the wood itself. Colour, for instance."

"It is certainly darker than the rest."

"So it is," He took the two pieces carrying the puttied hole, threw the rest on the heap, and addressed the landlady. "The Mr Harvey Challitt who occupied this room before Mr Kingscote, and who got into trouble for forgery, was the Mr Harvey Challitt who was himself robbed of diamonds a few months before on a staircase, wasn't he?"

"Yes, sir," Mrs Lamb replied in some bewilderment. "He certainly was that, on his own office stairs, chloroformed."

"Just so, and when they marched him away because of the forgery, Mr Kingscote changed into his rooms?"

"Yes, and very glad I was. It was bad enough to have the disgrace brought into the house, without the trouble of trying to get people to take his very rooms, and I thought—"

"Yes, yes, very awkward, very awkward!" Hewitt interrupted rather impatiently. "The man who took the rooms on Monday, now—you'd never seen him before, had you?"

"No, sir."

"Then is that anything like him?" Hewitt held a cabinet photograph before her.

"Why—why—law, yes, that's him!"

Hewitt dropped the photograph back into his breast pocket with a contented "Um," and picked up his hat. "I think we may soon be able to find that young gentleman for you, Mrs Lamb. He is not a very respectable young gentleman, and perhaps you are well rid of him, even as it is. Come, Brett," he added, "the day hasn't been wasted, after all."

We made towards the nearest telegraph office. On the way I said, "That puttied-up hole in the piece of wood seems to have influenced you. Is it an important link?"

"Well—yes," Hewitt answered, "it is. But all those other pieces are important, too."

"But why?"

"Because there are no holes in them." He looked quizzically at my wondering face, and laughed aloud. "Come," he said, "I won't puzzle you much longer. Here is the post-office. I'll send my wire, and then we'll go and dine at Luzatti's."

He sent his telegram, and we cabbed it to Luzatti's. Among actors, journalists, and others who know town and like a good dinner, Luzatti's is well known. We went upstairs for the sake of quietness, and took a table standing alone in a recess just inside the door. We ordered our dinner, and then Hewitt began:

"Now tell me what your conclusion is in this matter of the Ivy Cottage murder."

"Mine? I haven't one. I'm sorry I'm so very dull, but I really haven't."

"Come, I'll give you a point. Here is the newspaper account (torn sacrilegiously from my scrap-book for your benefit) of the robbery perpetrated on Harvey Challitt a few months before his forgery. Read it."

"Oh, but I remember the circumstances very well. He was carrying two packets of diamonds belonging to his firm downstairs to the office of another firm of diamond merchants on the ground-floor. It was a quiet time in the day, and halfway down he was seized on a dark landing, made insensible by chloroform, and robbed of the diamonds—five or six thousand pounds' worth altogether, of stones of various smallish individual values up to thirty pounds or so. He lay unconscious on the landing till one of the partners, noticing that he had been rather long gone, followed and found him. That's all, I think."

"Yes, that's all. Well, what do you make of it?"

"I'm afraid I don't quite see the connection with this case."

"Well, then, I'll give you another point. The telegram I've just sent releases information to the police, in consequence of which they will probably apprehend Harvey Challitt and his confederate Henry Gillard, alias Jones, for the murder of Gavin Kingscote. Now, then."

"Challitt! But he's in gaol already."

"Tut, tut, consider. Five years' penal was his dose, although for the first offence, because the forgery was of an extremely dangerous sort. You left Chelsea over three years ago yourself, and you told me that his difficulty occurred a year before. That makes four years, at least. Good conduct in prison brings a man out of a five year's sentence in that time or a little less, and, as a matter of fact, Challitt was released rather more than a week ago."

"Still, I'm afraid I don't see what you are driving at."

"Whose story is this about the diamond robbery from Harvey Challitt?"

"His own."

"Exactly. His own. Does his subsequent record make him look like a person whose stories are to be accepted without doubt or question?"

"Why, no. I think I see—no, I don't. You mean he stole them himself? I've a sort of dim perception of your drift now, but still I can't fix it. The whole thing's too complicated."

"It is a little complicated for a first effort, I admit, so I will tell you. This is the story. Harvey Challitt is an artful young man, and decides on a theft of his firm's diamonds. He first prepares a hiding-place somewhere near the stairs of his office, and when the opportunity arrives he puts the stones away, spills his chloroform, and makes a smell—possibly sniffs some, and actually goes off on the stairs, and the whole thing's done. He is carried into the office—the diamonds are gone. He tells of the attack on the stairs, as we have heard, and he is believed. At a suitable opportunity he takes his plunder from the hiding-place, and goes home to his lodgings. What is he to do with those diamonds? He can't sell them yet, because the robbery is publicly notorious, and all the regular jewel buyers know him.

"Being a criminal novice, he doesn't know any regular receiver of stolen goods, and if he did would prefer to wait and get full value by an ordinary sale. There will always be a danger of detection so long as the stones are not securely hidden, so he proceeds to hide them. He knows that if any suspicion were aroused his rooms would be searched in every likely place, so he looks for an unlikely place. Of course, he thinks of taking out a panel and hiding them behind that. But the idea is so obvious that it won't do; the police would certainly take those panels out to look behind them. Therefore he determines to hide them in the panels. See here"—he took the two pieces of wood with the filled hole from his tail pocket and opened his penknife—the putty near the surface is softer than that near the bottom of the hole; two different lots of putty, differently mixed, perhaps, have been used, therefore, presumably, at different times.

"But to return to Challitt. He makes holes with a centre-bit in different places on the panels, and in each hole he places a diamond, embedding it carefully in putty. He smooths the surface carefully flush with the wood, and then very carefully paints the place over, shading off the paint at the edges so as to leave no signs of a patch. He doesn't do the whole job at once, creating a noise and a smell of paint, but keeps on steadily, a few holes at a time, till in a little while the whole wainscoting is set with hidden diamonds, and every panel is apparently sound and whole."

"But, then—there was only one such hole in the whole lot."

Just so, and that very circumstance tells us the whole truth. Let me tell the story first—I'll explain the clue after. The diamonds lie hidden for a few months—he grows impatient. He wants the money, and he can't see a way of getting it. At last he determines to make a bolt and go abroad to sell his plunder. He knows he will want money for expenses, and that he may not be able to get rid of his diamonds at once. He also expects that his suddenly going abroad while the robbery is still in people's minds will bring suspicion on him in any case, so, in for a penny in for a pound, he commits a bold forgery, which, had it been successful, would have put him in funds and enabled him to leave the country with the stones. But the forgery is detected, and he is haled to prison, leaving the diamonds in their wainscot setting.

"Now we come to Gavin Kingscote. He must have been a shrewd fellow—the sort of man that good detectives are made of. Also he must have been pretty unscrupulous. He had his suspicions about the genuineness of the diamond robbery, and kept his eyes open. What indications he had to guide him we don't know, but living in the same house a sharp fellow on the look—out would probably see enough. At any rate, they led him to the belief that the diamonds were in the thief's rooms, but not among his movables, or they would have been found after the arrest. Here was his chance. Challitt was out of the way for years, and there was plenty of time to take the house to pieces if it were necessary. So he changed into Challitt's rooms.

"How long it took him to find the stones we shall never know. He probably tried many other places first, and, I expect, found the diamonds at last by pricking over the panels with a needle. Then came the problem of getting them out without attracting attention. He decided not to trust to the needle, which might possibly leave a stone or two undiscovered, but to split up each panel carefully into splinters so as to leave no part unexamined. Therefore he took measurements, and had a number of panels made by a joiner of the exact size and pattern of those in the room, and announced to his landlady his intention of painting her panels with a pretty design. This to account for the wet paint, and even for the fact of a panel being out of the wall, should she chance to bounce into the room at an awkward moment. All very clever, eh?"

"Very."

"Ah, he was a smart man, no doubt. Well, he went to work, taking out a panel, substituting a new one, painting it over, and chopping up the old one on the quiet, getting rid of the splinters out of doors when the booty had been extracted. The decoration progressed and the little heap of diamonds grew. Finally, he came to the last panel, but found that he had used all his new panels and hadn't one left for a substitute. It must have been at some time when it was difficult to get hold of the joiner—Bank Holiday, perhaps, or Sunday, and he was impatient. So he scraped the paint off, and went carefully over every part of the surface—experience had taught him by this that all the holes were of the same sort—and found one diamond. He took it out, refilled the hole with putty, painted the old panel and put it back. These are pieces of that old panel—the only old one of the lot.

"Nine men out of ten would have got out of the house as soon as possible after the thing was done, but he was a cool hand and stayed. That made the whole thing look a deal more genuine than if he had unaccountably cleared out as soon as he had got his room nicely decorated. I expect the original capital for those Stock Exchange operations we heard of came out of those diamonds. He stayed as long as suited him, and left when he set up housekeeping with a view to his wedding. The rest of the story is pretty plain. You guess it, of course?"

"Yes," I said, "I think I can guess the rest, in a general sort of way—except as to one or two points."

"It's all plain—perfectly. See here! Challitt, in gaol, determines to get those diamonds when he comes out. To do that without being suspected it will be necessary to hire the room. But he knows that he won't be able to do that himself, because the landlady, of course, knows him, and won't have an ex-convict in the house. There is no help for it; he must have a confederate, and share the spoil. So he makes the acquaintance of another convict, who seems a likely man for the job, and whose sentence expires about the same time as his own. When they come out, he arranges the matter with this confederate, who is a well-mannered (and pretty well-known) housebreaker, and the latter calls at Mrs Lamb's house to look for rooms. The very room itself happens to be to let, and of course it is taken, and Challitt (who is the invalid cousin) comes in at night muffled and unrecognizable.

"The decoration on the panel does not alarm them, because, of course, they suppose it to have been done on the old panels and over the old paint. Challitt tries the spots where diamonds were left—there are none—there is no putty even. Perhaps, think they, the panels have been shifted and interchanged in the painting, so they set to work and split them all up as we have seen, getting more desperate as they go on. Finally they realize that they are done, and clear out, leaving Mrs Lamb to mourn over their mischief.

"They know that Kingscote is the man who has forestalled them, because Gillard (or Jones), in his chat with the landlady, has heard all about him and his painting of the panels. So the next night they set off for Finchley. They get into Kingscote's garden and watch him let Campbell out. While he is gone, Challitt quietly steps through the French window into the smoking-room, and waits for him, Gillard remaining outside.

"Kingscote returns, and Challitt accuses him of taking the stones. Kingscote is contemptuous—doesn't care for Challitt, because he knows he is powerless, being the original thief himself; besides, knows there is no evidence, since the diamonds are sold and dispersed long ago. Challitt offers to divide the plunder with him—Kingscote laughs and tells him to go; probably threatens to throw him out, Challitt being the smaller man. Gillard, at the open window, hears this, steps in behind, and quietly knocks him on the head. The rest follows as a matter of course. They fasten the window and shutters, to exclude observation; turn over all the drawers, etc., in case the jewels are there; go to the best bedroom and try there, and so on. Failing (and possibly being disturbed after a few hours' search by the noise of the acquisitive gardener), Gillard, with the instinct of an old thief, determines they shan't go away with nothing, so empties Kingscote's pockets and takes his watch and chain and so on. They go out by the front door and shut it after them. Voilà tout."

I was filled with wonder at the prompt ingenuity of the man who in these few hours of hurried inquiry could piece together so accurately all the materials of an intricate and mysterious affair such as this; but more, I wondered where and how he had collected those materials.

"There is no doubt, Hewitt," I said, "that the accurate and minute application of what you are pleased to call your common sense has become something very like an instinct with you. What did you deduce from? You told me your conclusions from the examination of Ivy Cottage, but not how you arrived at them."

"They didn't leave me much material downstairs, did they? But in the bedroom, the two drawers which the thieves found locked were ransacked—opened probably with keys taken from the dead man. On the floor I saw a bent French nail; here it is. You see, it is twice bent at right angles, near the head and near the point, and there is the faint mark of the pliers that were used to bend it. It is a very usual burglars' tool, and handy in experienced hands to open ordinary drawer locks. Therefore, I knew that a professional burglar had been at work. He had probably fiddled at the drawers with the nail first, and then had thrown it down to try the dead man's keys.

"But I knew this professional burglar didn't come for a burglary, from several indications. There was no attempt to take plate, the first thing a burglar looks for. Valuable clocks were left on mantelpieces, and other things that usually go in an ordinary burglary were not disturbed. Notably, it was to be observed that no doors or windows were broken, or had been forcibly opened; therefore, it was plain that the thieves had come in by the French window of the smoking-room, the only entrance left open at the last thing. Therefore, they came in, or one did, knowing that Mr Kingscote was up, and being quite willing—presumably anxious—to see him. Ordinary burglars would have waited till he had retired, and then could have got through the closed French window as easily almost as if it were open, notwithstanding the thin wooden shutters, which would never stop a burglar for more than five minutes. Being anxious to see him, they—or again, one of them—presumably knew him. That they had come to get something was plain, from the ransacking. As, in the end, they did steal his money and watch, but did not take larger valuables, it was plain that they had no bag with them—which proves not only that they had not come to burgle, for every burglar takes his bag, but that the thing they came to get was not bulky. Still, they could easily have removed plate or clocks by rolling them up in a table-cover or other wrapper, but such a bundle, carried by well—dressed men, would attract attention—therefore it was probable that they were well dressed. Do I make it clear?"

"Quite—nothing seems simpler now it is explained—that's the way with difficult puzzles."

"There was nothing more to be got at the house. I had already in my mind the curious coincidence that the panels at Chelsea had been broken the very night before that of the murder, and determined to look at them in any case. I got from you the name of the man who had lived in the panelled room before Kingscote, and at once remembered it (although I said nothing about it) as that of the young man who had been chloroformed for his employer's diamonds. I keep things of that sort in my mind, you see—and, indeed, in my scrap-book. You told me yourself about his imprisonment, and there I was with what seemed now a hopeful case getting into a promising shape.

"You went on to prevent any setting to rights at Chelsea, and I made enquiries as to Challitt. I found he had been released only a few days before all this trouble arose, and I also found the name of another man who was released from the same establishment only a few days earlier. I knew this man (Gillard) well, and knew that nobody was a more likely rascal for such a crime as that at Finchley. On my way to Chelsea I called at my office, gave my clerk certain instructions, and looked up my scrap-book. I found the newspaper account of the chloroform business, and also a photograph of Gillard—I keep as many of these things as I can collect. What I did at Chelsea you know. I saw that one panel was of old wood and the rest new. I saw the hole in the old panel, and I asked one or two questions. The case was complete."

We proceeded with our dinner. Presently I said: "It all rests with the police now, of course?"

"Of course. I should think it very probable that Challitt and Gillard will be caught. Gillard, at any rate, is pretty well known. It will be rather hard on the surviving Kingscote, after engaging me, to have his dead brother's diamond transactions publicly exposed as a result, won't it? But it can't be helped. Fiat justitia, of course."

"How will the police feel over this?" I asked. "You've rather cut them out, eh?"

"Oh, the police are all right. They had not the information I had, you see; they knew nothing of the panel business. If Mrs Lamb had gone to Scotland Yard instead of to the policeman on the beat, perhaps I should never have been sent for."

The same quality that caused Martin Hewitt to rank as mere "common-sense" his extraordinary power of almost instinctive deduction, kept his respect for the abilities of the police at perhaps a higher level than some might have considered justified.

We sat some little while over our dessert, talking as we sat, when there occurred one of those curious conjunctions of circumstances that we notice again and again in ordinary life, and forget as often, unless the importance of the occasion fixes the matter in the memory. A young man had entered the dining-room, and had taken his seat at a corner table near the back window. He had been sitting there for some little time before I particularly observed him. At last he happened to turn his thin, pale face in my direction, and our eyes met. It was Challitt—the man we had been talking of!

I sprang to my feet in some excitement.

"That's the man!" I cried. "Challitt!"

Hewitt rose at my words, and at first attempted to pull me back. Challitt, in guilty terror, saw that we were between him and the door, and turning, leaped upon the sill of the open window, and dropped out. There was a fearful crash of broken glass below, and everybody rushed to the window.

Hewitt drew me through the door, and we ran downstairs. "Pity you let out like that," he said, as he went. "If you'd kept quiet we could have sent out for the police with no trouble. Never mind—can't help it."

Below, Challitt was lying in a broken heap in the midst of a crowd of waiters. He had crashed through a thick glass skylight and fallen, back downward, across the back of a lounge. He was taken away on a stretcher unconscious, and, in fact, died in a week in hospital from injuries to the spine.

During his periods of consciousness he made a detailed statement, bearing out the conclusions of Martin Hewitt with the most surprising exactness, down to the smallest particulars. He and Gillard had parted immediately after the crime, judging it safer not to be seen together. He had, he affirmed, endured agonies of fear and remorse in the few days since the fatal night at Finchley, and had even once or twice thought of giving himself up. When I so excitedly pointed him out, he knew at once that the game was up, and took the one desperate chance of escape that offered. But to the end he persistently denied that he had himself committed the murder, or had even thought of it till he saw it accomplished. That had been wholly the work of Gillard, who, listening at the window and perceiving the drift of the conversation, suddenly beat down Kingscote from behind with a life-preserver.

And so Harvey Challitt ended his life at the age of twenty-six.

Gillard was never taken. He doubtless left the country, and has probably since that time become "known to the police" under another name abroad. Perhaps he has even been hanged, and if he has been, there was no miscarriage of justice, no matter what the charge against him may have been.

II. — THE NICOBAR BULLION CASE

The whole voyage was an unpleasant one, and Captain Mackrie, of the Anglo-Malay Company's steamship Nicobar, had at last some excuse for the ill-temper that had made him notorious and unpopular in the company's marine staff. Although the fourth and fifth mates in the seclusion of their berth ventured deeper in their search for motives, and opined that the "old man" had made a deal less out of this voyage than usual; the company having lately taken to providing its own stores; so that "makings" were gone clean and "cumshaw" (which means commission in the trading lingo of the China seas) had shrunk small indeed. In confirmation they adduced the uncommonly long face of the steward (the only man in the ship satisfied with the skipper), whom the new regulations hit with the same blow. But indeed the steward's dolor might well be credited to the short passenger list, and the unpromising aspect of the few passengers in the eyes of a man accustomed to gauge one's tip-yielding capacity a month in advance. For the steward it was altogether the wrong time of year, the wrong sort of voyage, and certainly the wrong sort of passengers. So that doubtless the confidential talk of the fourth and fifth officers was mere youthful scandal. At any rate, the captain had prospect of a good deal in private trade home, for he had been taking curiosities and Japanese oddments aboard (plainly for sale in London) in a way that a third steward would have been ashamed of, and which, for a captain, was a scandal and an ignominy; and he had taken pains to insure well for the lot. These things the fourth and fifth mates often spoke of, and more than once made a winking allusion to, in the presence of the third mate and the chief engineer, who laughed and winked too, and sometimes said as much to the second mate, who winked without laughing; for of such is the tittle-tattle of shipboard.

The Nicobar was bound home with few passengers, as I have said, a small general cargo, and gold bullion to the value of £200,000—the bullion to be landed at Plymouth, as usual. The presence of this bullion was a source of much conspicuous worry on the part of the second officer, who had charge of the bullion-room. For this was his first voyage on his promotion from third officer, and the charge of £200,000 worth of gold bars was a thing he had not been accustomed to. The placid first officer pointed out to him that this wasn't the first shipment of bullion the world had ever known, by a long way, nor the largest. Also that every usual precaution was taken, and the keys were in the captain's cabin; so that he might reasonably be as easy in his mind as the few thousand other second officers who had had charge of hatches and special cargo since the world began. But this did not comfort Brasyer. He fidgeted about when off watch, considering and puzzling out the various means by which the bullion-room might be got at, and fidgeted more when on watch, lest somebody might be at that moment putting into practice the ingenious dodges he had thought of. And he didn't keep his fears and speculations to himself. He bothered the first officer with them, and when the first officer escaped he explained the whole thing at length to the third officer.

"Can't think what the company's about," he said on one such occasion to the first mate, "calling a tin-pot bunker like that a bullion-room."

"Skittles!" responded the first mate, and went on smoking.

"Oh, that's all very well for you who aren't responsible," Brasyer went on, "but I'm pretty sure something will happen some day; if not on this voyage on some other. Talk about a strong room! Why, what's it made of?"

"Three-eighths boiler plate."

"Yes, three-eighths boilerplate—about as good as a sixpenny tin money box. Why, I'd get through that with my grandmother's scissors!"

"All right; borrow 'em and get through. I would if I had a grandmother."

"There it is down below there out of sight and hearing, nice and handy for anybody who likes to put in a quiet hour at plate cutting from the coal bunker next door—always empty, because it's only a seven-ton bunker, not worth trimming. And the other side's against the steward's pantry. What's to prevent a man shipping as steward, getting quietly through while he's supposed to be bucketing about among his slops and his crockery, and strolling away with the plunder at the next port? And then there's the carpenter. He's always messing about somewhere below, with a bag full of tools. Nothing easier than for him to make a job in a quiet corner, and get through the plates."

"But then what's he to do with the stuff when he's got it? You can't take gold ashore by the hundredweight in your boots."

"Do with it. Why, dump it, of course. Dump it overboard in a quiet port and mark the spot. Come to that, he could desert clean at Port Said—what easier place?—and take all he wanted. You know what Port Said's like. Then there are the firemen—oh, anybody can do it!" And Brasyer moved off to take another peep under the hatchway.

The door of the bullion-room was fastened by one central patent lock and two padlocks, one above and one below the other lock. A day or two after the conversation recorded above, Brasyer was carefully examining and trying the lower of the padlocks with a key, when a voice immediately behind him asked sharply, "Well, sir, and what are you up to with that padlock?"

Brasyer started violently and looked round. It was Captain Mackrie.

"There's—that is—I'm afraid these are the same sort of padlocks as those in the carpenter's stores," the second mate replied, in a hurry of explanation. "I—I was just trying, that's all; I'm afraid the keys fit."

"Just you let the carpenter take care of his own stores, will you, Mr. Brasyer? There's a Chubb's lock there as well as the padlocks, and the key of that's in my cabin, and I'll take care doesn't go out of it without my knowledge. So perhaps you'd best leave off experiments till you're asked to make 'em, for your own sake. That's enough now," the captain added, as Brasyer appeared to be ready to reply; and he turned on his heel and made for the steward's quarters.

Brasyer stared after him ragefully. "Wonder what you want down here," he muttered under his breath. "Seems to me one doesn't often see a skipper as thick with the steward as that." And he turned off growling towards the deck above.

"Hanged if I like that steward's pantry stuck against the side of the bullion-room," he said later in the day to the first officer. "And what does a steward want with a lot of boiler-maker's tools aboard? You know he's got them."

"In the name of the prophet, rats!" answered the first mate, who was of a less fussy disposition. "What a fatiguing creature you are, Brasyer! Don't you know the man's a boiler-maker by regular trade, and has only taken to stewardship for the last year or two? That sort of man doesn't like parting with his tools, and as he's a widower, with no home ashore, of course he has to carry all his traps aboard. Do shut up, and take your proper rest like a Christian. Here, I'll give you a cigar; it's all right—Burman; stick it in your mouth, and keep your jaw tight on it."

But there was no soothing the second officer. Still he prowled about the after orlop deck, and talked at large of his anxiety for the contents of the bullion-room. Once again, a few days later, as he approached the iron door, he was startled by the appearance of the captain coming, this time, from the steward's pantry. He fancied he had heard tapping, Brasyer explained, and had come to investigate. But the captain turned him back with even less ceremony than before, swearing he would give charge of the bullion-room to another officer if Brasyer persisted in his eccentricities. On the first deck the second officer was met by the carpenter, a quiet, sleek, soft-spoken man, who asked him for the padlock and key he had borrowed from the stores during the week. But Brasyer put him off, promising to send it back later. And the carpenter trotted away to a job he happened to have, singularly enough, in the hold, just under the after orlop deck, and below the floor of the bullion-room.

As I have said, the voyage was in no way a pleasant one. Everywhere the weather was at its worst, and scarce was Gibraltar passed before the Lascars were shivering in their cotton trousers, and the Seedee boys were buttoning tight such old tweed jackets as they might muster from their scanty kits. It was January. In the Bay the weather was tremendous, and the Nicobar banged and shook and pitched distractedly across in a howling world of thunderous green sea, washed within and without, above and below. Then, in the Chops, as night fell, something went, and there was no more steerageway, nor, indeed, anything else but an aimless wallowing. The screw had broken.

The high sea had abated in some degree, but it was still bad. Such sail as the steamer carried, inadequate enough, was set, and shift was made somehow to worry along to Plymouth—or to Falmouth if occasion better served—by that means. And so the Nicobar beat across the Channel on a rather better, though anything but smooth, sea, in a black night, made thicker by a storm of sleet, which turned gradually to snow as the hours advanced.

The ship laboured slowly ahead, through a universal blackness that seemed to stifle. Nothing but a black void above, below, and around, and the sound of wind and sea; so that one coming before a deck-light was startled by the quiet advent of the large snowflakes that came like moths as it seemed from nowhere. At four bells—two in the morning—a foggy light appeared away on the starboard bow—it was the Eddystone light—and an hour or two later, the exact whereabouts of the ship being a thing of much uncertainty, it was judged best to lay her to till daylight. No order had yet been given, however, when suddenly there were dim lights over the port quarter, with a more solid blackness beneath them. Then a shout and a thunderous crash, and the whole ship shuddered, and in ten seconds had belched up every living soul from below. The Nicobar's voyage was over—it was a collision.

The stranger backed off into the dark, and the two vessels drifted apart, though not till some from the Nicobar had jumped aboard the other. Captain Mackrie's presence of mind was wonderful, and never for a moment did he lose absolute command of every soul on board. The ship had already begun to settle down by the stern and list to port. Life-belts were served out promptly. Fortunately there were but two women among the passengers, and no children. The boats were lowered without a mishap, and presently two strange boats came as near as they dare from the ship (a large coasting steamer, it afterwards appeared) that had cut into the Nicobar. The last of the passengers were being got off safely, when Brayser, running anxiously to the captain, said:—

"Can't do anything with that bullion, can we, sir? Perhaps a box or two—"

"Oh, damn the bullion!" shouted Captain Mackrie. "Look after the boat, sir, and get the passengers off. The insurance companies can find the bullion for themselves."

But Brasyer had vanished at the skipper's first sentence. The skipper turned aside to the steward as the crew and engine-room staff made for the remaining boats, and the two spoke quietly together. Presently the steward turned away as if to execute an order, and the skipper continued in a louder tone:—

"They're the likeliest stuff, and we can but drop 'em, at worst. But be slippy—she won't last ten minutes."

She lasted nearly a quarter of an hour. By that time, however, everybody was clear of her, and the captain in the last boat was only just near enough to see the last of her lights as she went down.

II

The day broke in a sulky grey, and there lay the Nicobar, in ten fathoms, not a mile from the shore, her topmasts forlornly visible above the boisterous water. The sea was rough all that day, but the snow had ceased, and during the night the weather calmed considerably. Next day Lloyd's agent was steaming about in a launch from Plymouth, and soon a salvage company's tug came up and lay by the emerging masts. There was every chance of raising the ship as far as could be seen, and a diver went down from the salvage tug to measure the breach made in the Nicobar's side, in order that the necessary oak planking or sheeting might be got ready for covering the hole, preparatory to pumping and raising. This was done in a very short time, and the necessary telegrams having been sent, the tug remained in its place through the night, and prepared for the sending down of several divers on the morrow to get out the bullion as a commencement.

Just at this time Martin Hewitt happened to be engaged on a case of some importance and delicacy on behalf of Lloyd's Committee, and was staying for a few days at Plymouth. He heard the story of the wreck, of course, and speaking casually with Lloyd's agent as to the salvage work just beginning, he was told the name of the salvage company's representative on the tug, Mr. Percy Merrick—a name he immediately recognised as that of an old acquaintance of his own. So that on the day when the divers were at work in the bullion-room of the sunken Nicobar, Hewitt gave himself a holiday, and went aboard the tug about noon.

Here he found Merrick, a big, pleasant man of thirty-eight or so. He was very glad to see Hewitt, but was a great deal puzzled as to the results of the morning's work on the wreck. Two cases of gold bars were missing.

"There was £200,000 worth of bullion on board," he said, "that's plain and certain. It was packed in forty cases, each of £5,000 value. But now there are only thirty-eight cases! Two are gone clearly. I wonder what's happened?"

"I suppose your men don't know anything about it?" asked Hewitt.

"No, they're all right. You see, it's impossible for them to bring anything up without its being observed, especially as they have to be unscrewed from their diving-dresses here on deck. Besides, bless you, I was down with them."

"Oh! Do you dive yourself, then?"

"Well, I put the dress on sometimes, you know, for any such special occasion as this. I went down this morning. There was no difficulty in getting about on the vessel below, and I found the keys of the bullion-room just where the captain said I would, in his cabin. But the locks were useless, of course, after being a couple of days in salt water. So we just burgled the door with crowbars, and then we saw that we might have done it a bit more easily from outside. For that coasting-steamer cut clean into the bunker next the bullion-room, and ripped open the sheet of boiler-plate dividing them."

"The two missing cases couldn't have dropped out that way, of course?"

"Oh, no. We looked, of course, but it would have been impossible. The vessel has a list the other way—to starboard—and the piled cases didn't reach as high as the torn part. Well, as I said, we burgled the door, and there they were, thirty-eight sealed bullion cases, neither more nor less, and they're down below in the after-cabin at this moment. Come and see."

Thirty-eight they were; pine cases bound with hoop-iron and sealed at every joint, each case about eighteen inches by a foot, and six inches deep. They were corded together, two and two, apparently for convenience of transport.

"Did you cord them like this yourself?" asked Hewitt.

"No, that's how we found 'em. We just hooked 'em on a block and tackle, the pair at a time, and they hauled 'em up here aboard the tug."

"What have you done about the missing two—anything?"

"Wired off to headquarters, of course, at once. And I've sent for Captain Mackrie—he's still in the neighbourhood, I believe—and Brasyer, the second officer, who had charge of the bullion-room. They may possibly know something. Anyway, one thing's plain. There were forty cases at the beginning of the voyage, and now there are only thirty-eight."

There was a pause; and then Merrick added, "By the bye, Hewitt, this is rather your line, isn't it? You ought to look up these two cases."

Hewitt laughed. "All right," he said; "I'll begin this minute if you'll commission me."

"Well," Merrick replied slowly, "of course I can't do that without authority from headquarters. But if you've nothing to do for an hour or so there is no harm in putting on your considering cap, is there? Although, of course, there's nothing to go upon as yet. But you might listen to what Mackrie and Brasyer have to say. Of course I don't know, but as it's a £10,000 question probably it might pay you, and if you do see your way to anything I'd wire and get you Commissioned at once."

There was a tap at the door and Captain Mackrie entered. "Mr. Merrick?" he said interrogatively, looking from one to another.

"That's myself, sir," answered Merrick.

"I'm Captain Mackrie, of the Nicobar. You sent for me, I believe. Something wrong with the bullion I'm told, isn't it?"

Merrick explained matters fully. "I thought perhaps you might be able to help us, Captain Mackrie. Perhaps I have been wrongly informed as to the number of cases that should have been there?"

"No; there were forty right enough. I think though—perhaps I might be able to give you a sort of hint "— and Captain Mackrie looked hard at Hewitt.

"This is Mr. Hewitt, Captain Mackrie," Merrick interposed. "You may speak as freely as you please before him. In fact, he's sort of working on the business, so to speak."

"Well," Mackrie said, "if that's so, speaking between ourselves, I should advise you to turn your attention to Brasyer. He was my second officer, you know, and had charge of the stuff."

"Do you mean," Hewitt asked, "that Mr. Brasyer might give us some useful information?"

Mackrie gave an ugly grin. "Very likely he might," he said, "if he were fool enough. But I don't think you'd get much out of him direct. I meant you might watch him."

"What, do you suppose he was concerned in any way with the disappearance of this gold?"

"I should think—speaking, as I said before, in confidence and between ourselves—that it's very likely indeed. I didn't like his manner all through the voyage."

"Why?"

"Well, he was so eternally cracking on about his responsibility, and pretending to suspect the stokers and the carpenter, and one person and another, of trying to get at the bullion cases—that that alone was almost enough to make one suspicious. He protested so much, you see. He was so conscientious and diligent himself, and all the rest of it, and everybody else was such a desperate thief, and he was so sure there would be some of that bullion missing some day that—that—well, I don't know if I express his manner clearly, but I tell you I didn't like it a bit. But there was something more than that. He was eternally smelling about the place, and peeping in at the steward's pantry—which adjoins the bullion-room on one side, you know—and nosing about in the bunker on the other side. And once I actually caught him fitting keys to the padlocks—keys he'd borrowed from the carpenter's stores. And every time his excuse was that he fancied he heard somebody else trying to get in to the gold, or something of that sort; every time I caught him below on the orlop deck that was his excuse—happened to have heard something or suspected something or somebody every time. Whether or not I succeed in conveying my impressions to you, gentlemen, I can assure you that I regarded his whole manner and actions as very suspicious throughout the voyage, and I made up my mind I wouldn't forget it if by chance anything did turn out wrong. Well, it has, and now I've told you what I've observed. It's for you to see if it will lead you anywhere."

"Just so," Hewitt answered. "But let me fully understand. Captain Mackrie. You say that Mr. Brasyer had charge of the bullion-room, but that he was trying keys on it from the carpenter's stores. Where were the legitimate keys then?"

"In my cabin. They were only handed out when I knew what they were wanted for. There was a Chubb's lock between the two padlocks, but a duplicate wouldn't have been hard for Brasyer to get. He could easily have taken a wax impression of my key when he used it at the port where we took the bullion aboard."

"Well, and suppose he had taken these boxes, where do you think he would keep them?"

Mackrie shrugged his shoulders and smiled. "Impossible to say," he replied. "He might have hidden 'em somewhere on board, though I don't think that's likely. He'd have had a deuce of a job to land them at Plymouth, and would have had to leave them somewhere while he came on to London. Bullion is always landed at Plymouth, you know, and if any were found to be missing, then the ship would be overhauled at once, every inch of her; so that he'd have to get his plunder ashore somehow before the rest of the gold was unloaded—almost impossible. Of course, if he's done that it's somewhere below there now, but that isn't likely. He'd be much more likely to have 'dumped' it—dropped it overboard at some well-known spot in a foreign port, where he could go later on and get it. So that you've a deal of scope for search, you see. Anywhere under water from here to Yokohama;" and Captain Mackrie laughed.

Soon afterward he left, and as he was leaving a man knocked at the cabin door and looked in to say that Mr. Brasyer was on board. "You'll be able to have a go at him now," said the captain. "Good-day."

"There's the steward of the Nicobar there too, sir," said the man after the captain had gone, "and the carpenter."

"Very well, we'll see Mr. Brasyer first," said Merrick, and the man vanished. "It seems to have got about a bit," Merrick went on to Hewitt. "I only sent for Brasyer, but as these others have come, perhaps they've got something to tell us."

Brasyer made his appearance, overflowing with information. He required little assurance to encourage him to speak openly before Hewitt, and he said again all he had so often said before on board the Nicobar. The bullion-room was a mere tin box, the whole thing was as easy to get at as anything could be, he didn't wonder in the least at the loss—he had prophesied it all along.

The men whose movements should be carefully watched, he said, were the captain and the steward. "Nobody ever heard of a captain and a steward being so thick together before," he said. "The steward's pantry was next against the bullion-room, you know, with nothing but that wretched bit of three-eighths boiler plate between. You wouldn't often expect to find the captain down in the steward's pantry, would you, thick as they might be. Well, that's where I used to find him, time and again. And the steward kept boiler-makers' tools there! That I can swear to. And he's been a boiler-maker, so that, likely as not, he could open a joint somewhere and patch it up again neatly so that it wouldn't be noticed. He was always messing about down there in his pantry, and once I distinctly heard knocking there, and when I went down to see, whom should I meet? Why, the skipper, coming away from the place himself, and he bully-ragged me for being there and sent me on deck. But before that he bully-ragged me because I had found out that there were other keys knocking about the place that fitted the padlocks on the bullion-room door. Why should he slang and threaten me for looking after these things and keeping my eye on the bullion-room, as was my duty? But that was the very thing that he didn't like. It was enough for him to see me anxious about the gold to make him furious. Of course his character for meanness and greed is known all through the company's service—he'll do anything to make a bit."

"But have you any positive idea as to what has become of the gold?"

"Well," Brasyer replied, with a rather knowing air, "I don't think they've dumped it."

"Do you mean you think it's still in the vessel—hidden somewhere?"

"No, I don't. I believe the captain and the steward took it ashore, one case each, when we came off in the boats."

"But wouldn't that be noticed?"

"It needn't be, on a black night like that. You see, the parcels are not so big—look at them, a foot by a foot and a half by six inches or so, roughly. Easily slipped under a big coat or covered up with anything. Of course they're a bit heavy—eighty or ninety pounds apiece altogether—but that's not much for a strong man to carry—especially in such a handy parcel, on a black night, with no end of confusion on. Now you just look here—I'll tell you something. The skipper went ashore last in a boat that was sent out by the coasting steamer that ran into us. That ship's put into dock for repairs and her crew are mostly having an easy time ashore. Now I haven't been asleep this last day or two, and I had a sort of notion there might be some game of this sort on, because when I left the ship that night I thought we might save a little at least of the stuff, but the skipper wouldn't let me go near the bullion-room, and that seemed odd. So I got hold of one of the boat's crew that fetched the skipper ashore, and questioned him quietly—pumped him, you know—and he assures me that the skipper did have a rather small, heavy sort of parcel with him. What do you think of that? Of course, in the circumstances, the man couldn't remember any very distinct particulars, but he thought it was a sort of square wooden case about the size I've mentioned. But there's something more." Brasyer lifted his forefinger and then brought it down on the table before him—"something more. I've made inquiries at the railway station and I find that two heavy parcels were sent off yesterday to London—deal boxes wrapped in brown paper, of just about the right size. And the paper got torn before the things were sent off, and the clerk could see that the boxes inside were fastened with hoop-iron—like those!" and the second officer pointed triumphantly to the boxes piled at one side of the cabin.

"Well done!" said Hewitt. "You're quite a smart detective. Did you find out who brought the parcels, and who they were addressed to?"

"No, I couldn't get quite as far as that. Of course the clerk didn't know the names of the senders, and not knowing me, wouldn't tell me exactly where the parcels were going. But I got quite chummy with him after a bit, and I'm going to meet him presently—he has the afternoon off, and we're going for a stroll. I'll find something more, I'll bet you!"

"Certainly," replied Hewitt, "find all you can—it may be very important. If you get any valuable information you'll let us know at once, of course. Anything else, now?"

"No, I don't think so; but I think what I've told you is pretty well enough for the present, eh? I'll let you know some more soon."

Brasyer went, and Norton, the steward of the old ship, was brought into the cabin. He was a sharp-eyed, rather cadaverous-looking man, and he spoke with sepulchral hollowness. He had heard, he said, that there was something wrong with the chests of bullion, and came on board to give any information he could. It wasn't much, he went on to say, but the smallest thing might help. If he might speak strictly confidentially he would suggest that observation be kept on Wickens, the carpenter. He (Norton) didn't want to be uncharitable, but his pantry happened to be next the bullion-room, and he had heard Wickens at work for a very long time just below—on the under side of the floor of the bullion-room, it seemed to him, although, of course, he might have been mistaken. Still, it was very odd that the carpenter always seemed to have a job just at that spot. More, it had been said—and he (Norton) believed it to be true—that Wickens, the carpenter, had in his possession, and kept among his stores, keys that fitted the padlocks on the bullion-room door. That, it seemed to him, was a very suspicious circumstance. He didn't know anything more definite, but offered his ideas for what they were worth, and if his suspicions proved unfounded nobody would be more pleased than himself. But—but—and the steward shook his head doubtfully.

"Thank you, Mr. Norton," said Merrick, with a twinkle in his eye; "we won't forget what you say. Of course, if the stuff is found in consequence of any of your information, you won't lose by it."

The steward said he hoped not, and he wouldn't fail to keep his eye on the carpenter. He had noticed Wickens was in the tug, and he trusted that if they were going to question him they would do it cautiously, so as not to put him on his guard. Merrick promised they would.

"By the bye, Mr. Norton," asked Hewitt, "supposing your suspicions to be justified, what do you suppose the carpenter would do with the bullion?"

"Well, sir," replied Norton, "I don't think he'd keep it on the ship. He'd probably dump it somewhere."

The steward left, and Merrick lay back in his chair and guffawed aloud. "This grows farcical," he said, "simply farcical. What a happy family they must have been aboard the Nicobar! And now here's the captain watching the second officer, and the second officer watching the captain and the steward, and the steward watching the carpenter! It's immense. And now we're going to see the carpenter. Wonder whom he suspects?"

Hewitt said nothing, but his eyes twinkled with intense merriment, and presently the carpenter was brought into the cabin.

"Good-day to you, gentlemen," said the carpenter in a soft and deferential voice, looking from one to the other. "Might I 'ave the honour of addressin' the salvage gentlemen?"

"That's right," Merrick answered, motioning him to a seat. "This is the salvage shop, Mr. Wickens. What can we do for you?"

The carpenter coughed gently behind his hand. "I took the liberty of comin', gentlemen, consekins o' 'earin' as there was some bullion missin'. P'raps I'm wrong."

"Not at all. We haven't found as much as we expected, and I suppose by this time nearly everybody knows it. There are two cases wanting. You can't tell us where they are, I suppose?"

"Well, sir, as to that—no. I fear I can't exactly go as far as that. But if I am able to give vallable information as may lead to recovery of same, I presoom I may without offence look for some reasonable small recognition of my services?"

"Oh, yes," answered Merrick, "that'll be all right, I promise you. The company will do the handsome thing, of course, and no doubt so will the underwriters."

"Presoomin' I may take that as a promise—among gentlemen "—this with an emphasis—"I'm willing to tell something."

"It's a promise, at any rate as far as the company's concerned," returned Merrick. "I'll see it's made worth your while—of course, providing it leads to anything."

"Purvidin' that, sir, o' course. Well, gentlemen, my story ain't a long one. All I've to say was what I 'card on board, just before she went down. The passengers was off, and the crew was gettin' into the other boats when the skipper turns to the steward an' speaks to him quiet-like, not observin', gentlemen, as I was agin 'is elbow, so for to say. "'Ere, Norton,' 'e sez, or words to that effeck, 'why shouldn't we try gettin' them things ashore with us—you know, the cases—eh? I've a notion we're pretty close inshore,' 'e sez, 'and there's nothink of a sea now. You take one, anyway, and I'll try the other,' 'e says, 'but don't make a flourish.' Then he sez, louder, 'cos o' the steward goin' off, 'They're the likeliest stuff, and at worst we can but drop 'em. But look sharp,' 'e says. So then I gets into the nearest boat, and that's all I 'eard."

"That was all?" asked Hewitt, watching the man's face sharply.

"All?" the carpenter answered with some surprise. "Yes, that was all; but I think it's pretty well enough, don't you? It's plain enough what was meant—him and the steward was to take two cases, one apiece, on the quiet, and they was the likeliest stuff aboard, as he said himself. And now there's two cases o' bullion missin'. Ain't that enough?"

The carpenter was not satisfied till an exact note had been made of the captain's words. Then after Merrick's promise on behalf of the company had been renewed, Wickens took himself off.

"Well," said Merrick, grinning across the table at Hewitt, "this is a queer go, isn't it? What that man says makes the skipper's case look pretty fishy, doesn't it? What he says, and what Brasyer says, taken together, makes a pretty strong case—I should say makes the thing a certainty. But what a business! It's likely to be a bit serious for some one, but it's a rare joke in a way. Wonder if Brasyer will find out anything more? Pity the skipper and steward didn't agree as to whom they should pretend to suspect. That's a mistake on their part."

"Not at all," Hewitt replied. "If they are conspiring, and know what they're about, they will avoid seeming to be both in a tale. The bullion is in bars, I understand?"

"Yes, five bars in each case; weight, I believe, sixteen pounds to a bar."

"Let me see," Hewitt went on, as he looked at his watch; "it is now nearly two o'clock. I must think over these things if I am to do anything in the case. In the meantime, if it could be managed, I should like enormously to have a turn under water in a diving-dress. I have always had a curiosity to see under the sea. Could it be managed now?"

"Well," Merrick responded, "there's not much fun in it, I can assure you; and it's none the pleasanter in this weather. You'd better have a try later in the year if you really want to—unless you think you can learn anything about this business by smelling about on the Nicobar down below?"

Hewitt raised his eyebrows and pursed his lips.

"I might spot something," he said; "one never knows. And if I do anything in a case I always make it a rule to see and hear everything that can possibly be seen or heard, important or not. Clues lie where least expected. But beyond that, probably I may never have another chance of a little experience in a diving-dress. So if it can be managed I'd be glad."

"Very well, you shall go, if you say so. And since it's your first venture, I'll come down with you myself. The men are all ashore, I think, or most of them. Come along."

Hewitt was put in woollens and then in indiarubbers. A leaden-soled boot of twenty pounds' weight was strapped on each foot, and weights were hung on his back and chest.

"That's the dress that Gullen usually has," Merrick remarked. "He's a very smart fellow; we usually send him first to make measurements and so on. An excellent man, but a bit too fond of the diver's lotion."

"What's that?" asked Hewitt.

"Oh, you shall try some if you like, afterwards. It's a bit too heavy for me; rum and gin mixed, I think."

A red nightcap was placed on Martin Hewitt's head, and after that a copper helmet, secured by a short turn in the segmental screw joint at the neck. In the end he felt a vast difficulty in moving at all. Merrick had been meantime invested with a similar rig-out, and then each was provided with a communication cord and an incandescent electric lamp. Finally, the front window was screwed on each helmet, and all was ready.

Merrick went first over the ladder at the side, and Hewitt with much difficulty followed. As the water closed over his head, his sensations altered considerably. There was less weight to carry; his arms in particular felt light, though slow in motion. Down, down they went slowly, and all round about it was fairly light, but once on the sunken vessel and among the lower decks, the electric lamps were necessary enough. Once or twice Merrick spoke, laying his helmet against Hewitt's for the purpose, and instructing him to keep his air-pipe, life-line, and lamp connection from fouling something at every step. Here and there shadowy swimming shapes came out of the gloom, attracted by their lamps, to dart into obscurity again with a twist of the tail. The fishes were exploring the Nicobar. The hatchway of the lower deck was open, and down this they passed to the orlop deck. A little way along this they came to a door standing open, with a broken lock hanging to it. It was the door of the bullion-room, which had been forced by the divers in the morning.

Merrick indicated by signs how the cases had been found piled on the floor. One of the sides of the room of thin steel was torn and thrust in the length of its whole upper half, and when they backed out of the room and passed the open door they stood in the great breach made by the bow of the strange coasting vessel. Steel, iron, wood, and everything stood in rents and splinters, and through the great gap they looked out into the immeasurable ocean. Hewitt put up his hand and felt the edge of the bullion-room partition where it had been torn. It was just such a tear as might have been made in cardboard.

They regained the upper deck, and Hewitt, placing his helmet against his companion's, told him that he meant to have a short walk on the ocean bed. He took to the ladder again, where it lay over the side, and Merrick followed him.

The bottom was of that tough, slimy sort of clay-rock that is found in many places about our coasts, and was dotted here and there with lumps of harder rock and clumps of curious weed. The two divers turned at the bottom of the ladder, walked a few steps, and looked up at the great hole in the Nicobar's side. Seen from here it was a fearful chasm, laying open hold, orlop, and lower deck.

Hewitt turned away, and began walking about. Once or twice he stood and looked thoughtfully at the ground he stood on, which was fairly flat. He turned over with his foot a whitish, clean-looking stone about as large as a loaf. Then he wandered on slowly, once or twice stopping to examine the rock beneath him, and presently stooped to look at another stone nearly as large as the other, weedy on one side only, standing on the edge of a cavity in the claystone. He pushed the stone into the hole, which it filled, and then he stood up.

Merrick put his helmet against Hewitt's, and shouted—

"Satisfied now? Seen enough of the bottom?"

"In a moment!" Hewitt shouted back; and he straightway began striding out in the direction of the ship. Arrived at the bows, he turned back to the point he started from, striding off again from there to the white stone he had kicked over, and from there to the vessel's side again. Merrick watched him in intense amazement, and hurried, as well as he might, after the light of Hewitt's lamp. Arrived for the second time at the bows of the ship, Hewitt turned and made his way along the side to the ladder, and forthwith ascended, followed by Merrick. There was no halt at the deck this time, and the two made there way up and up into the lighter water above, and so to the world of air.

On the tug, as the men were unscrewing them from there waterproof prisons, Merrick asked Hewitt—

"Will you try the 'lotion' now?"

"No," Hewitt replied, "I won't go quite so far as that. But I will have a little whisky, if you've any in the cabin. And give me a pencil and a piece of paper."

These things were brought, and on the paper Martin Hewitt immediately wrote a few figures and kept it in his hand.

"I might easily forget those figures," he observed.

Merrick wondered, but said nothing.

Once more comfortably in the cabin, and clad in his usual garments, Hewitt asked if Merrick could produce a chart of the parts thereabout.

"Here you are," was the reply, "coast and all. Big enough, isn't it? I've already marked the position of the wreck on it in pencil. She lies pointing north by east as nearly exact as anything."

"As you've begun it," said Hewitt, "I shall take the liberty of making a few more pencil marks on this." And with that he spread out the crumpled note of figures, and began much ciphering and measuring. Presently he marked certain points on a spare piece of paper, and drew through them two lines forming an angle. This angle he transferred to the chart, and, placing a ruler over one leg of the angle, lengthened it out till it met the coast-line.

"There we are," he said musingly. "And the nearest village to that is Lostella—indeed, the only coast village in that neighbourhood." He rose. "Bring me the sharpest-eyed person on board," he said; "that is, if he were here all day yesterday."

"But what's up? What's all this mathematical business over? Going to find that bullion by rule of three?"

Hewitt laughed. "Yes, perhaps," he said, "but Where's your sharp look-out? I want somebody who can tell me everything that was visible from the deck of this tug all day yesterday."

"Well, really I believe the very sharpest chap is the boy. He's most annoyingly observant sometimes. I'll send for him."

He came—a bright, snub-nosed, impudent-looking young ruffian.

"See here, my boy," said Merrick, "polish up your wits and tell this gentleman what he asks."

"Yesterday," said Hewitt, "no doubt you saw various pieces of wreckage floating about?"

"Yessir."

"What were they?"

"Hatch-gratings mostly—nothin' much else. There's some knockin' about now."

"I saw them. Now, remember. Did you set a hatch-grating floating yesterday that was different from the others? A painted one, for instance—those out there now are not painted, you know."

"Yessir, I see a little white 'un painted, bobbin' about away beyond the foremast of the Nicobar."

"You're sure of that?"

"Certain sure, sir—it was the only painted thing floatin'. And to-day it's washed away somewheres."

"So I noticed. You're a smart lad. Here's a shilling for you—keep your eyes open and perhaps you'll find a good many more shillings before you're an old man. That's all."

The boy disappeared, and Hewitt turned to Merrick and said, "I think you may as well send that wire you spoke of. If I get the commission I think I may recover that bullion. It may take some little time, or, on the other hand, it may not. If you'll write the telegram at once, I'll go in the same boat as the messenger. I'm going to take a walk down to Lostella now—it's only two or three miles along the coast, but it will soon be getting dark."

"But what sort of a clue have you got? I didn't—"

"Never mind," replied Hewitt, with a chuckle. "Officially, you know, I've no right to a clue just yet—I'm not commissioned. When I am I'll tell you everything."

Hewitt was scarcely ashore when he was seized by the excited Brasyer. "Here you are," he said. "I was coming aboard the tug again. I've got more news. You remember I said I was going out with that railway clerk this afternoon, and meant pumping him? Well, I've done it and rushed away—don't know what he'll think's up. As we were going along we saw Norton, the steward, on the other side of the way, and the clerk recognised him as one of the men who brought the cases to be sent off; the other was the skipper, I've no doubt, from his description. I played him artfully, you know, and then he let out that both the cases were addressed to Mackrie at his address in London! He looked up the entry, he said, after I left when I first questioned him, feeling curious. That's about enough, I think, eh? I'm off to London now—I believe Mackrie's going to-night. I'll have him! Keep it dark!" And the zealous second officer dashed off without waiting for a reply. Hewitt looked after him with an amused smile, and turned off towards Lostella.

III

It was about eleven the next morning when Merrick received the following note, brought by a boatman:—

"Dear Merrick,—Am I commissioned? If not, don't trouble, but if I am, be just outside Lostella, at the turning before you come to the Smack Inn, at two o'clock. Bring with you a light cart, a policeman—or two perhaps will be better—and a man with a spade. There will probably be a little cabbage-digging. Are you fond of the sport?—Yours, Martin Hewitt.

"P.S.—Keep all your men aboard; bring the spade artist from the town."

Merrick was off in a boat at once. His principals had replied to his telegram after Hewitt's departure the day before, giving him a free hand to do whatever seemed best. With some little difficulty he got the policemen, and with none at all he got a light cart and a jobbing man with a spade. Together they drove off to the meeting-place.

It was before the time, but Martin Hewitt was there, waiting. "You're quick," he said, "but the sooner the better. I gave you the earliest appointment I thought you could keep, considering what you had to do."

"Have you got the stuff, then?" Merrick asked anxiously.

"No, not exactly yet. But I've got this," and Hewitt held up the point of his walking-stick. Protruding half an inch or so from it was the sharp end of a small gimlet, and in the groove thereof was a little white wood, such as commonly remains after a gimlet has been used.

"Why, what's that?"

"Never mind. Let us move along—I'll walk. I think we're about at the end of the job—it's been a fairly lucky one, and quite simple. But I'll explain after."

Just beyond the Smack Inn, Hewitt halted the cart, and all got down. They looped the horse's reins round a hedge-stake and proceeded the small remaining distance on foot, with the policemen behind, to avoid a premature scare. They turned up a lane behind a few small and rather dirty cottages facing the sea, each with its patch of kitchen garden behind. Hewitt led the way to the second garden, pushed open the small wicket gate and walked boldly in, followed by the others.

Cabbages covered most of the patch, and seemed pretty healthy in their situation, with the exception of half a dozen—singularly enough, all together in a group. These were drooping, yellow, and wilted, and towards these Hewitt straightway walked. "Dig up those wilted cabbages," he said to the jobbing man. "They're really useless now. You'll probably find something else six inches down or so."

The man struck his spade into the soft earth, wherein it stopped suddenly with a thud. But at this moment a gaunt, slatternly woman, with a black eye, a handkerchief over her head, and her skirt pinned up in front, observing the invasion from the back door of the cottage, rushed out like a maniac and attacked the party valiantly with a broom. She upset the jobbing man over his spade, knocked off one policeman's helmet, lunged into the other's face with her broom, and was making her second attempt to hit Hewitt (who had dodged), when Merrick caught her firmly by the elbows from behind, pressed them together, and held her. She screamed, and people came from other cottages and looked on. "Peter! Peter!" the woman screamed, "come 'ee, come'ee here! Davey! They're come!"

A grimy child came to the cottage door, and seeing the woman thus held, and strangers in the garden, set up a piteous howl. Meantime the digger had uncovered two wooden boxes, each eighteen inches long or so, bound with hoop-iron and sealed. One had been torn partly open at the top, and the broken wood roughly replaced. When this was lifted, bars of yellow metal were visible within.

The woman still screamed vehemently, and struggled. The grimy child retreated, and then there appeared at the door, staggering hazily and rubbing his eyes, a shaggy, unkempt man, in shirt and trousers. He looked stupidly at the scene before him, and his jaw dropped.

"Take that man," cried Hewitt. "He's one!" And the policeman promptly took him, so that he had handcuffs on his wrists before he had collected his faculties sufficiently to begin swearing.

Hewitt and the other policeman entered the cottage. In the lower two rooms there was nobody. They climbed the few narrow stairs, and in the front room above they found another man, younger, and fast asleep. "He's the other," said Hewitt. "Take him." And this one was handcuffed before he woke.

Then the recovered gold was put into the cart, and with the help of the village constable, who brought his own handcuffs for the benefit and adornment of the lady with the broom, such a procession marched out of Lostella as had never been dreamed of by the oldest inhabitant in his worst nightmare, nor recorded in the whole history of Cornwall.

"Now," said Hewitt, turning to Merrick, "we must have that fellow of yours—what's his name—Gullen, isn't it? The one that went down to measure the hole in the ship. You've kept him aboard, of course?"

"What, Gullen?" exclaimed Merrick. "Gullen? Well, as a matter of fact he went ashore last night and hasn't come back. But you don't mean to say—"

"I do," replied Hewitt. "And now you've lost him."

IV

"But tell me all about it now we've a little time to ourselves," asked Merrick an hour or two later, as they sat and smoked in the after-cabin of the salvage tug. "We've got the stuff, thanks to you, but I don't in the least see how they got it, nor how you found it out."

"Well, there didn't seem to be a great deal either way in the tales told by the men from the Nicobar. They cancelled one another out, so to speak, though it seemed likely that there might be something in them in one or two respects. Brasyer, I could see, tried to prove too much. If the captain and the steward were conspiring to rob the bullion-room, why should the steward trouble to cut through the boiler-plate walls when the captain kept the keys in his cabin? And if the captain had been stealing the bullion, why should he stop at two cases when he had all the voyage to operate in and forty cases to help himself to? Of course the evidence of the carpenter gave some colour to the theory, but I think I can imagine a very reasonable explanation of that.

"You told me, of course, that you were down with the men yourself when they opened the bullion-room door and got out the cases, so that there could be no suspicion of them. But at the same time you told me that the breach in the Nicobar's side had laid open the bullion-room partition, and that you might more easily have got the cases out that way. You told me, of course, that the cases couldn't have fallen out that way because of the list of the vessel, the position of the rent in the boiler-plate, and so on. But I reflected that the day before a diver had been down alone—in fact, that his business had been with the very hole that extended partly to the bullion-room: he had to measure it. That diver might easily have got at the cases through the breach. But then, as you told me, a diver can't bring things up from below unobserved. This diver would know this, and might therefore hide the booty below. So that I made up my mind to have a look under water before I jumped to any conclusion.

"I didn't think it likely that he had hidden the cases, mind you. Because he would have had to dive again to get them, and would have been just as awkwardly placed in fetching them to the light of day then as ever. Besides, he couldn't come diving here again in the company's dress without some explanation. So what more likely than that he would make some ingenious arrangement with an accomplice, whereby he might make the gold in some way accessible to him?

"We went under water. I kept my eyes open, and observed, among other things, that the vessel was one of those well-kept 'swell' ones on which all the hatch gratings and so on are in plain oak or teak, kept holystoned. This (with the other things) I put by in my mind in case it should be useful. When we went over the side and looked at the great gap, I saw that it would have been quite easy to get at the broken bullion-room partition from outside."

"Yes," remarked Merrick, "it would be no trouble at all. The ladder goes down just by the side of the breach, and any one descending by that might just step off at one side on to the jagged plating at the level of the after orlop, and reach over into the bullion safe."

"Just so. Well, next I turned my attention to the sea-bed, which I was extremely pleased to see was of soft, slimy claystone. I walked about a little, getting farther and farther away from the vessel as I went, till I came across that clean stone which I turned over with my foot. Do you remember?"

"Yes."

"Well, that was noticeable. It was the only clean, bare stone to be seen. Every other was covered with a green growth, and to most clumps of weed clung. The obvious explanation of this was that the stone was a new-comer—lately brought from dry land—from the shingle on the sea-shore, probably, since it was washed so clean. Such a stone could not have come a mile out to sea by itself. Somebody had brought it in a boat and thrown it over, and whoever did it didn't take all that trouble for nothing. Then its shape told a tale; it was something of the form, rather exaggerated, of a loaf—the sort that is called a 'cottage'—the most convenient possible shape for attaching to a line and lowering. But the line had gone, so somebody must have been down there to detach it. Also it wasn't unreasonable to suppose that there might have been a hook on the end of that line. This, then, was a theory. Your man had gone down alone to take his measurement, had stepped into the broken side, as you have explained he could, reached into the bullion-room, and lifted the two cases. Probably he unfastened the cord, and brought them out one at a time for convenience in carrying. Then he carried the cases, one at a time, as I have said, over to that white stone which lay there sunk with the hook and line attached by previous arrangement with some confederate. He detached the rope from the stone—it was probably fixed by an attached piece of cord, tightened round the stone with what you call a timber-hitch, easily loosened—replaced the cord round the two cases, passed the hook under the cord, and left it to be pulled up from above. But then it could not have been pulled up there in broad daylight, under your very noses. The confederates would wait till night. That meant that the other end of the rope was attached to some floating object, so that it might be readily recovered. The whole arrangement was set one night to be carried away the next."

"But why didn't Gullen take more than two cases?"

"He couldn't afford to waste the time, in the first place. Each case removed meant another journey to and from the vessel, and you were waiting above for his measurements. Then he was probably doubtful as to weight. Too much at once wouldn't easily be drawn up, and might upset a small boat.

"Well, so much for the white stone. But there was more; close by the stone I noticed (although I think you didn't) a mark in the claystone. It was a triangular depression or pit, sharp at the bottom—just the hole that would be made by the sharp impact of the square corner of a heavy box, if shod with iron, as the bullion cases are. This was one important thing. It seemed to indicate that the boxes had not been lifted directly up from the seabed, but had been dragged sideways—at all events at first—so that a sharp corner had turned over and dug into the claystone! I walked a little farther and found more indications—slight scratches, small stones displaced, and so on, that convinced me of this, and also pointed out the direction in which the cases had been dragged. I followed the direction, and presently arrived at another stone, rather smaller than the clean one. The cases had evidently caught against this, and it had been displaced by their momentum, and perhaps by a possible wrench from above. The green growth covered the part which had been exposed to the water, and the rest of the stone fitted the hole beside it, from which it had been pulled. Clearly these things were done recently, or the sea would have wiped out all the traces in the soft claystone. The rest of what I did under water of course you understood."

"I suppose so: you took the bearings of the two stones in relation to the ship by pacing the distances."

"That is so. I kept the figures in my head till I could make a note of them, as you saw, on paper. The rest was mere calculation. What I judged had happened was this. Gullen had arranged with somebody, identity unknown, but certainly somebody with a boat at his disposal, to lay the line, and take it up the following night. Now anything larger than a rowing boat could not have got up quite so close to you in the night (although your tug was at the other end of the wreck) without a risk of being seen. But no rowing boat could have dragged those cases forcibly along the bottom; they would act as an anchor to it. Therefore this was what had happened. The thieves had come in a large boat—a fishing smack, lugger, or something of that sort—with a small boat in tow. The sailing boat had lain to at a convenient distance, in the direction in which it was afterwards to go, so as to save time if observed, and a man had put off quietly in the small boat to pick up the float, whatever it was. There must have been a lot of slack line on this for the purpose, as also for the purpose of allowing the float to drift about fairly freely, and not attract attention by remaining in one place. The man pulled off to the sailing boat, and took the float and line aboard. Then the sailing boat swung off in the direction of home, and the line was hauled in with the plunder at the end of it."

"One would think you had seen it all—or done it," Merrick remarked, with a laugh.

"Nothing else could have happened, you see. That chain of events is the only one that will explain the circumstances. A rapid grasp of the whole circumstances and a perfect appreciation of each is more than half the battle in such work as this. Well, you know I got the exact bearings of the wreck on the chart, worked out from that the lay of the two stones with the scratch marks between, and then it was obvious that a straight line drawn through these and carried ahead would indicate, approximately, at any rate, the direction the thieves' vessel had taken. The line fell on the coast close by the village of Lostella— indeed that was the only village for some few miles either way. The indication was not certain, but it was likely, and the only one available, therefore it must be followed up."

"And what about the painted hatch? How did you guess that?"

"Well, I saw there were hatch-gratings belonging to the Nicobar floating about, and it seemed probable that the thieves would use for a float something similar to the other wreckage in the vicinity, so as not to attract attention. Nothing would be more likely than a hatch-grating. But then, in small vessels, such as fishing-luggers and so on, fittings are almost always painted—they can't afford to be such holystoning swells as those on the Nicobar. So I judged the grating might be painted, and this would possibly have been noticed by some sharp person. I made the shot, and hit. The boy remembered the white grating, which had gone—' washed away,' as he thought. That was useful to me, as you shall see.

"I made off toward Lostella. The tide was low and it was getting dusk when I arrived. A number of boats and smacks were lying anchored on the beach, but there were few people to be seen. I began looking out for smacks with white-painted fittings in them. There are not so many of these among fishing vessels—brown or red is more likely, or sheer colourless dirt over paint unrecognisable. There were only two that I saw last night. The first might have been the one I wanted, but there was nothing to show it. The second was the one. She was half-decked and had a small white-painted hatch. I shifted the hatch and found a long line, attached to the grating at one end and carrying a hook at the other! They had neglected to unfasten their apparatus—perhaps had an idea that there might be a chance of using it again in a few days. I went to the transom and read the inscription, 'Rebecca. Peter and David Garthew, Lostella.' Then my business was to find the Garthews.

"I wandered about the village for some little time, and presently got hold of a boy. I made a simple excuse for asking about the Garthews—wanted to go for a sail to-morrow. The boy, with many grins, confided to me that both of the Garthews were 'on the booze.' I should find them at the Smack Inn, where they had been all day, drunk as fiddlers. This seemed a likely sort of thing after the haul they had made. I went to the Smack Inn, determined to claim old friendship with the Garthews, although I didn't know Peter from David. There they were—one sleepy drunk, and the other loving and crying drunk. I got as friendly as possible with them under the circumstances, and at closing time stood another gallon of beer and carried it home for them, while they carried each other. I took cafe to have a good look round in the cottage. I even helped Peter's 'old woman'—the lady with the broom—to carry them up to bed. But nowhere could I see anything that looked like a bullion-case or a hiding-place for one. So I came away, determined to renew my acquaintance in the morning, and to carry it on as long as might be necessary; also to look at the garden in the daylight for signs of burying. With that view I fixed that little gimlet in my walking-stick, as you saw.

"This morning I was at Lostella before ten, and took a look at the Garthews' cabbages. It seemed odd that half a dozen, all in a clump together, looked withered and limp, as though they had been dug up hastily, the roots broken, perhaps, and then replanted. And altogether these particular cabbages had a dissipated, leaning-different-ways look, as though they had been on the loose with the Garthews. So, seeing a grubby child near the back door of the cottage, I went towards him, walking rather unsteadily, so as, if I were observed, to favour the delusion that I was not yet quite got over last night's diversions. 'Hullo, my b-boy,' I said, 'hullo, li'l b-boy, look here,' and I plunged my hand into my trousers' pocket and brought it out full of small change. Then, making a great business of selecting him a penny, I managed to spill it all over the dissipated cabbages. It was easy then, in stooping to pick up the change, to lean heavily on my stick and drive it through the loose earth. As I had expected, there was a box below. So I gouged away with my walking-stick while I collected my coppers, and finally swaggered off, after a few civil words with the 'old woman,' carrying with me evident proof that it was white wood recently buried there. The rest you saw for yourself. I think you and I may congratulate each other on having dodged that broom. It hit all the others."

"What I'm wild about," said Merrick, "is having let that scoundrel Gullen get off. He's an artful chap, without a doubt. He saw us go over the side, you know, and after you had gone he came into the cabin for some instructions. Your pencil notes and the chart were on the table, and no doubt he put two and two together (which was more than I could, not knowing what had happened), and concluded to make himself safe for a bit. He had no leave that night—he just pulled away on the quiet. Why didn't you give me the tip to keep him?"

"That wouldn't have done. In the first place, there was no legal evidence to warrant his arrest, and ordering him to keep aboard would have aroused his suspicions. I didn't know at the time how many days, or weeks, it would take me to find the bullion, if I ever found it, and in that time Gullen might have communicated in some way with his accomplices, and so spoilt the whole thing. Yes, certainly he seems to have been fairly smart in his way. He knew he would probably be sent down first, as usual, alone to make measurements, and conceived his plan and made his arrangements forthwith."

"But now what I want to know is what about all those Nicobar people watching and suspecting one another? More especially what about the cases the captain and the steward are said to have fetched ashore?"

Hewitt laughed. "Well," he said, "as to that, the presence of the bullion seems to have bred all sorts of mutual suspicion on board the ship. Brasyer was over-fussy, and his continual chatter started it probably, so that it spread like an infection. As to the captain and the steward, of course I don't know anything but that their rescued cases were bullion cases. Probably they were doing a little private trading—it's generally the case when captain and steward seem unduly friendly for their relative positions—and perhaps the cases contained something specially valuable: vases or bronzes from Japan, for instance; possibly the most valuable things of the size they had aboard. Then, if they had insured their things. Captain Mackrie (who has the reputation of a sharp and not very scrupulous man) might possibly think it rather a stroke of business to get the goods and the insurance money too, which would lead him to keep his parcels as quiet as possible. But that's as it may be."

The case was much as Hewitt had surmised. The zealous Brasyer, posting to London in hot haste after Mackrie, spent some days in watching him. At last the captain and the steward with their two boxes took a cab and went to Bond Street, with Brasyer in another cab behind them. The two entered a shop, the window of which was set out with rare curiosities and much old silver and gold. Brasyer could restrain himself no longer. He grabbed a passing policeman, and rushed with him into the shop. There they found the captain and the steward with two small packing cases opened before them, trying to sell—a couple of very ancient-looking Japanese bronze figures, of that curious old workmanship and varied colour of metal that in genuine examples mean nowadays high money value.

Brasyer vanished: there was too much chaff for him to live through in the British mercantile marine after this adventure. The fact was, the steward had come across the bargain, but had not sufficient spare cash to buy, so he called in the aid of the captain, and they speculated in the bronzes as partners. There was much anxious inspection of the prizes on the way home, and much discussion as to the proper price to ask. Finally, it was said, they got three hundred pounds for the pair.

Now and again Hewitt meets Merrick still. Sometimes Merrick says, "Now, I wonder after all whether or not some of those Nicobar men who were continually dodging suspiciously about that bullion-room did mean having a dash at the gold if there were a chance?" And Hewitt replies, "I wonder."

III. — THE HOLFORD WILL CASE

At one time, in common, perhaps, with most people, I took a sort of languid, amateur interest in questions of psychology, and was impelled thereby to plunge into the pages of the many curious and rather abstruse books which attempt to deal with phenomena of mind, soul and sense. Three things of the real nature of which, I am convinced, no man will ever learn more than we know at present—which is nothing.

From these I strayed into the many volumes of Transactions of the Psychical Research Society, with an occasional by-excursion into mental telepathy and theosophy; the last, a thing whereof my Philistine intelligence obstinately refused to make head or tail.

It was while these things were occupying part of my attention that I chanced to ask Hewitt whether, in the course of his divers odd and out-of-the-way experiences, he had met with any such weird adventures as were detailed in such profusion in the books of "authenticated" spooks, doppelgangers, poltergeists, clairvoyance, and so forth.

"Well," Hewitt answered, with reflection, "I haven't been such a wallower in the uncanny as some of the worthy people who talk at large in those books of yours, and, as a matter of fact, my little adventures, curious as some of them may seem, have been on the whole of the most solid and matter-of-fact description. One or two things have happened that perhaps your 'psychical' people might be interested in, but they've mostly been found to be capable of a disappointingly simple explanation. One case of some genuine psychological interest, however, I have had; although there's nothing even in that which isn't a matter of well-known scientific possibility." And he proceeded to tell me the story that I have set down here, as well as I can, from recollection.

I think I have already said, in another place, that Hewitt's professional start as a private investigator dated from his connection with the famous will case of Bartley v. Bartley and others, in which his then principals, Messrs. Crellan, Hunt & Crellan, chiefly through his exertions established their extremely high reputation as solicitors. It was ten years or so after this case that Mr. Crellan senior—the head of the firm—retired into private life, and by an odd chance Hewitt's first meeting with him after that event was occasioned by another will difficulty.

These were the terms of the telegram that brought Hewitt again into personal relations with his old principal:—

"CAN YOU RUN DOWN AT ONCE ON A MATTER OF PRIVATE BUSINESS? I WILL BE AT GUILDFORD TO MEET ELEVEN THIRTY-FIVE FROM WATERLOO. IF LATER OR PREVENTED PLEASE WIRE. CRELLAN."

The day and the state of Hewitt's engagements suited, and there was full half an hour to catch the train. Taking, therefore, the small travelling-bag that always stood ready packed in case of any sudden excursion that presented the possibility of a night from home, he got early to Waterloo, and by half-past twelve was alighting at Guildford Station. Mr. Crellan, a hale, white-haired old gentleman, wearing gold-rimmed spectacles, was waiting with a covered carriage.

"How d'ye do, Mr. Hewitt, how d'ye do?" the old gentleman exclaimed as soon as they met, grasping Hewitt's hand, and hurrying him toward the carriage. "I'm glad you've come, very glad. It isn't raining, and you might have preferred something more open, but I brought the brougham because I want to talk privately. I've been vegetating to such an extent for the last few years down here that any little occurrence out of the ordinary excites me, and I'm sure I couldn't have kept quiet till we had got indoors. It's been bad enough, keeping the thing to myself, already."

The door shut, and the brougham started. Mr. Crellan laid his hand on Hewitt's knee, "I hope," he said, "I haven't dragged you away from any important business?"

"No," Hewitt replied, "you have chosen a most excellent time. Indeed, I did think of making a small holiday to-day, but your telegram—"

"Yes, yes. Do you know, I was almost ashamed of having sent it after it had gone. Because, after all, the matter is, probably, really a very simple sort of affair that you can't possibly help me in. A few years ago I should have thought nothing of it, nothing at all. But as I have told you, I've got into such a dull, vegetable state of mind since I retired and have nothing to do that a little thing upsets me, and I haven't mental energy enough to make up my mind to go to dinner sometimes. But you're an old friend, and I'm sure you'll forgive my dragging you all down here on a matter that will, perhaps, seem ridiculously simple to you, a man in the thick of active business. If I hadn't known you so well I wouldn't have had the impudence to bother you. But never mind all that. I'll tell you.

"Do you ever remember my speaking of an intimate friend, a Mr. Holford? No. Well, it's a long time ago, and perhaps I never happened to mention him. He was a most excellent man—old fellow, like me, you know; two or three years older, as a matter of fact. We were chums many years ago; in fact, we lodged in the same house when I was an articled clerk and he was a student at Guy's. He retired from the medical profession early, having come into a fortune, and came down here to live at the house we're going to; as a matter of fact, Wedbury Hall.

"When I retired I came down and took up my quarters not far off, and we were a very excellent pair of old chums till last Monday—the day before yesterday—when my poor old friend died.. He was pretty well in years—seventy-three—and a man can't live for ever. But I assure you it has upset me terribly, made a greater fool of me than ever, in fact, just when I ought to have my wits about me.

"The reason I particularly want my wits just now, and the reason I have requisitioned yours, is this: that I can't find poor old Holford's will. I drew it up for him years ago, and by it I was appointed his sole executor. I am perfectly convinced that he cannot have destroyed it, because he told me everything concerning his affairs. I have always been his only adviser, in fact, and I'm sure he would have consulted me as to any change in his testamentary intentions before he made it. Moreover, there are reasons why I know he could not have wished to die intestate."

"Which are?" queried Hewitt as Mr. Crellan paused in his statement.

"Which are these: Holford was a widower, with no children of his own. His wife, who has been dead nearly fifteen years now, was a most excellent woman, a model wife, and would have been a model mother if she had been one at all. As it was she adopted a little girl, a poor little soul who was left an orphan at two years of age. The child's father, an unsuccessful man of business of the name of Garth, maddened by a sudden and ruinous loss, committed suicide, and his wife died of the shock occasioned by the calamity.

"The child, as I have said, was taken by Mrs. Holford and made a daughter of, and my old friend's daughter she has been ever since, practically speaking. The poor old fellow couldn't possibly have been more attached to a daughter of his own, and on her part she couldn't possibly have been a better daughter than she was. She stuck by him night and day during his last illness, until she became rather ill herself, although of course there was a regular nurse always in attendance.

"Now, in his will, Mr. Holford bequeathed rather more than half of his very large property to this Miss Garth; that is to say, as residuary legatee, her interest in the will came to about that. The rest was distributed in various ways. Holford had largely spent the leisure of his retirement in scientific pursuits. So there were a few legacies to learned societies; all his servants were remembered; he left me a certain number of his books; and there was a very fair sum of money for his nephew, Mr. Cranley Mellis, the only near relation of Mr. Holford's still living. So that you see what the loss of this will may mean. Miss Garth, who was to have taken the greater part of her adoptive father's property, will not have one shilling's worth of claim on the estate and will be turned out into the world without a cent. One or two very old servants will be very awkwardly placed, too, with nothing to live on, and very little prospect of doing more work."

"Everything will go to this nephew," said Hewitt, "of course?"

"Of course. That is unless I attempt to prove a rough copy of the will which I may possibly have by me. But even if I have such a thing and find it, long and costly litigation would be called for, and the result would probably be all against us."

"You say you feel sure Mr. Holford did not destroy the will himself?"

"I am quite sure he would never have done so without telling me of it; indeed, I am sure he would have consulted me first. Moreover, it can never have been his intention to leave Miss Garth utterly unprovided for; it would be the same thing as disinheriting his only daughter."

"Did you see him frequently?"

"There's scarcely been a day when I haven't seen him since I have lived down here. During his illness—it lasted a month—I saw him every day."

"And he said nothing of destroying his will?"

"Nothing at all. On the contrary, soon after his first seizure—indeed, on the first visit at which I found him in bed—he said, after telling me how he felt, 'Everything's as I want it, you know, in case I go under.' That seemed to me to mean his will was still as he desired it to be."

"Well, yes, it would seem so. But counsel on the other side (supposing there were another side) might quite as plausibly argue that he meant to die intestate, and had destroyed his will so that everything should be as he wanted it, in that sense. But what do you want me to do—find the will?"

"Certainly, if you can. It seemed to me that you, with your clever head, might be able to form a better judgment than I as to what has happened and who is responsible for it. Because if the will has been taken away, some one has taken it."

"It seems probable. Have you told any one of your difficulty?"

"Not a soul. I came over as soon as I could after Mr. Holford's death, and Miss Garth gave me all the keys, because, as executor, the case being a peculiar one, I wished to see that all was in order, and, as you know, the estate is legally vested in the executor from the death of the testator, so that I was responsible for everything; although, of course, if there is no will I'm not executor. But I thought it best to keep the difficulty to myself till I saw you."

"Quite right. Is this Wedbury Hall?"

The brougham had passed a lodge gate, and approached, by a wide drive, a fine old red brick mansion carrying the heavy stone dressings and copings distinctive of early eighteenth century domestic architecture.

"Yes," said Mr. Crellan, "this is the place. We will go straight to the study, I think, and then I can explain details."

The study told the tale of the late Mr. Holford's habits and interests. It was half a library, half a scientific laboratory: pathological curiosities in spirits, a retort or two, test tubes on the writing-table, and a fossilized lizard mounted in a case, balanced the many shelves and cases of books disposed about the walls. In a recess between two book-cases stood a heavy, old-fashioned mahogany bureau.

"Now it was in that bureau," Mr. Crellan explained, indicating it with his finger, "that Mr. Holford kept every document that was in the smallest degree important or valuable. I have seen him at it a hundred times, and he always maintained it was as secure as any iron safe. That may not have been altogether the fact, but the bureau is certainly a tremendously heavy and strong one. Feel it."

Hewitt took down the front and pulled out a drawer that Mr. Crellan unlocked for the purpose.

"Solid Spanish mahogany an inch thick," was his verdict, "heavy, hard, and seasoned; not the sort of thing you can buy nowadays. Locks, Chubb's patent, early pattern, but not easily to be picked by anything short of a blast of gunpowder. If there are no marks on this bureau it hasn't been tampered with."

"Well," Mr. Crellan pursued, "as I say, that was where Mr. Holford kept his will. I have often seen it when we have been here together, and this was the drawer, the top on the right, that he kept it in. The will was a mere single sheet of foolscap, and was kept, folded of course, in a blue envelope."

"When did you yourself last actually see the will?"

"I saw it in my friend's hand two days before he took to his bed. He merely lifted it in his hand to get at something else in the drawer, replaced it, and locked the drawer again."

"Of course there are other drawers, bureaux, and so on, about the place. You have examined them carefully, I take it?"

"I've turned out ever possible receptacle for that will in the house, I positively assure you, and there isn't a trace of it."

"You've thought of secret drawers, I suppose?"

"Yes. There are two in the bureau which I always knew of. Here they are." Mr. Crellan pressed his thumb against a partition of the pigeonholes at the back of the bureau and a strip of mahogany flew out from below, revealing two shallow drawers with small ivory catches in lieu of knobs. "Nothing there at all. And this other, as I have said, was the drawer where the will was kept. The other papers kept in the same drawer are here as usual."

"Did anybody else know where Mr. Holford kept his will?"

"Everybody in the house, I should think. He was a frank, above-board sort of man. His adopted daughter knew, and the butler knew, and there was absolutely no reason why all the other servants shouldn't know; probably they did."

"First," said Hewitt, "we will make quite sure there are no more secret drawers about this bureau. Lock the door in case anybody comes."

Hewitt took out every drawer of the bureau, and examined every part of each before he laid it aside. Then he produced a small pair of silver callipers and an ivory pocket-rule and went over every inch of the heavy framework, measuring, comparing, tapping, adding, and subtracting dimensions. In the end he rose to his feet satisfied. "There is most certainly nothing concealed there," he said.

The drawers were put back, and Mr. Crellan suggested lunch. At Hewitt's suggestion it was brought to the study.

"So far," Hewitt said, "we arrive at this: either Mr. Holford has destroyed his will, or he has most effectually concealed it, or somebody has stolen it. The first of these possibilities you don't favour."

"I don't believe it is a possibility for a moment. I have told you why; and I knew Holford so well, you know. For the same reasons I am sure he never concealed it."

"Very well, then. Somebody has stolen it. The question is, who?"

"That is so."

"It seems to me that every one in this house had a direct and personal interest in preserving that will. The servants have all something left them, you say, and without the will that goes, of course. Miss Garth has the greatest possible interest in the will. The only person I have heard of as yet who would benefit by its loss or destruction would be the nephew, Mr. Mellis. There are no other relatives, you say, who would benefit by intestacy?"

"Not one."

"Well, what do you think yourself, now? Have you any suspicions?"

Mr. Crellan shrugged his shoulders. "I've no more right to suspicions than you have, I suppose," he said. "Of course, if there are to be suspicions they can only point one way. Mr. Mellis is the only person who can gain by the disappearance of this will."

"Just so. Now, what do you know of him?"

"I don't know much of the young man," Mr. Crellan said slowly. "I must say I never particularly took to him. He is rather a clever fellow, I believe. He was called to the bar some time ago, and afterwards studied medicine, I believe, with the idea of priming himself for a practice in medical jurisprudence. He took a good deal of interest in my old friend's researches, I am told—at any rate he said he did; he may have been thinking of his uncle's fortune. But they had a small tiff on some medical question. I don't know exactly what it was, but Mr. Holford objected to something—a method of research or something of that kind—as being dangerous and unprofessional. There was no actual rupture between them, you understand, but Mellis's visits slacked off, and there was a coolness."

"Where is Mr. Mellis now?"

"In London, I believe."

"Has he been in this house between the day you last saw the will in that drawer and yesterday, when you failed to find it?"

"Only once. He came to see his uncle two days before his death—last Saturday, in fact. He didn't stay long."

"Did you see him?"

"Yes."

"What did he do?"

"Merely came into the room for a few minutes—visitors weren't allowed to stay long—spoke a little to his uncle, and went back to town."

"Did he do nothing else, or see anybody else?"

"Miss Garth went out of the room with him as he left, and I should think they talked for a little before he went away, to judge by the time she was gone; but I don't know."

"You are sure he went then?"

"I saw him in the drive as I looked from the window."

"Miss Garth, you say, has kept all the keys since the beginning of Mr. Holford's illness?"

"Yes, until she gave them up to me yesterday. Indeed, the nurse, who is rather a peppery customer, and was jealous of Miss Garth's presence in the sick room all along, made several difficulties about having to go to her for everything."

"And there is no doubt of the bureau having been kept locked all the time?"

"None at all. I have asked Miss Garth that—and, indeed, a good many other things—without saying why I wanted the information."

"How are Mr. Mellis and Miss Garth affected toward one another—are they friendly?"

"Oh, yes. Indeed, some while ago I rather fancied that Mellis was disposed to pay serious addresses in that quarter. He may have had a fancy that way, or he may have been attracted by the young lady's expectations. At any rate, nothing definite seems to have come of it as yet. But I must say—between ourselves, of course—I have more than once noticed a decided air of agitation, shyness perhaps, in Miss Garth when Mr. Mellis has been present. But, at any rate, that scarcely matters. She is twenty-four years of age now, and can do as she likes. Although, if I had anything to say in the matter—well, never mind."

"You, I take it, have known Miss Garth along time?"

"Bless you, yes. Danced her on my knee twenty years ago. I've been her 'Uncle Leonard' all her life."

"Well, I think we must at least let Miss Garth know of the loss of the will. Perhaps, when they have cleared away these plates, she will come here for a few minutes."

"I'll go and ask her," Mr. Crellan answered, and having rung the bell, proceeded to find Miss Garth.

Presently he returned with the lady. She was a slight, very pale young woman; no doubt rather pretty in ordinary, but now not looking her best. She was evidently worn and nervous from anxiety and want of sleep, and her eyes were sadly inflamed. As the wind slammed a loose casement behind her she started nervously, and placed her hand to her head.

"Sit down at once, my dear," Mr. Crellan said; "sit down. This is Mr. Martin Hewitt, whom I have taken the liberty of inviting down here to help me in a very important matter. The fact is, my dear," Mr. Crellan added gravely, "I can't find your poor father's will."

Miss Garth was not surprised. "I thought so," she said mildly, "when you asked me about the bureau yesterday."

"Of course I need not say, my dear, what a serious thing it may be for you if that will cannot be found. So I hope you'll try and tell Mr. Hewitt here anything he wants to know as well as you can, without forgetting a single thing. I'm pretty sure that he will find it for us if it is to be found."

"I understand, Miss Garth," Hewitt asked, "that the keys of that bureau never left your possession during the whole time of Mr. Holford's last illness, and that the bureau was kept locked?"

"Yes, that is so."

"Did you ever have occasion to go to the bureau yourself?"

"No, I have not touched it."

"Then you can answer for it, I presume, that the bureau was never unlocked by any one from the time Mr. Holford placed the keys in your hands till you gave them to Mr. Crellan?"

"Yes, I am sure of that."

"Very good. Now is there any place on the whole premises that you can suggest where this will may possibly be hidden?"

"There is no place that Mr. Crellan doesn't know of, I'm sure."

"It is an old house, I observe," Hewitt pursued. "Do you know of any place of concealment in the structure—any secret doors, I mean, you know, or sliding panels, or hollow door frames, and so forth?"

Miss Garth shook her head. "There is not a single place of the sort you speak of in the whole building, so far as I know," she said, "and I have lived here almost all my life."

"You knew the purport of Mr. Holford's will, I take it, and understand what its loss may mean to yourself?"

"Perfectly."

"Now I must ask you to consider carefully. Take your mind back to two or three days before Mr. Holford's illness began, and tell me if you can remember any single fact, occurrence, word, or hint from that day to this in any way bearing on the will, or anything connected with it?"

Miss Garth shook her head thoughtfully. "I can't remember the thing being mentioned by anybody, except perhaps by the nurse, who is rather a touchy sort of woman, and once or twice took it upon herself to hint that my recent anxiety was chiefly about my poor father's money. And that once, when I had done some small thing for him, my father—I have always called him father, you know—said that he wouldn't forget it, or that I should be rewarded, or something of that sort. Nothing else that I can remember in the remotest degree concerned the will."

"Mr. Mellis said nothing about it, then?"

Miss Garth changed colour slightly, but answered, "No, I only saw him to the door."

"Thank you, Miss Garth, I won't trouble you any further just now. But if you can remember anything more in the course of the next few hours it may turn out to be of great service."

Miss Garth bowed and withdrew. Mr. Crellan shut the door behind her and returned to Hewitt. "That doesn't carry us much further," he said. "The more certain it seems that the will cannot have been got at, the more difficult our position is from a legal point of view. What shall we do now?"

"Is the nurse still about the place?"

"Yes, I believe so."

"Then I'll speak to her."

The nurse came in response to Mr. Crellan's summons: a sharp-featured, pragmatical woman of forty-five. She took the seat offered her, and waited for Hewitt's questions.

"You were in attendance on Mr. Holford, I believe, Mrs. Turton, since the beginning of his last illness?"

"Since October 24th."

"Were you present when Mr. Mellis came to see his uncle last Saturday?"

"Yes."

"Can you tell me what took place?"

"As to what the gentleman said to Mr. Holford," the nurse replied, bridling slightly, "of course I don't know anything, it not being my business and not intended for my ears. Mr. Crellan was there, and knows as much as I do, and so does Miss Garth. I only know that Mr. Mellis stayed for a few minutes and then went out of the room with Miss Garth."

"How long was Miss Garth gone?"

"I don't know, ten minutes or a quarter of an hour, perhaps."

"Now Mrs. Turton, I want you to tell me in confidence—it is very important—whether you, at any time, heard Mr. Holford during his illness say anything of his wishes as to how his property was to be left in case of his death?"

The nurse started and looked keenly from Hewitt to Mr. Crellan and back again.

"Is it the will you mean?" she asked sharply.

"Yes. Did he mention it?"

"You mean you can't find the will, isn't that it?"

"Well, suppose it is, what then?"

"Suppose won't do," the nurse answered shortly; "I do know something about the will, and I believe you can't find it."

"I'm sure, Mrs. Turton, that if you know anything about the will you will tell Mr. Crellan in the interests of right and justice."

"And who's to protect me against the spite of those I shall offend if I tell you?"

Mr. Crellan interposed.

"Whatever you tell us, Mrs. Turton," he said, "will be held in the strictest confidence, and the source of our information shall not be divulged. For that I give you my word of honour. And, I need scarcely add, I will see that you come to no harm by anything you may say."

"Then the will is lost. I may understand that?"

Hewitt's features were impassive and impenetrable. But in Mr. Crellan's disturbed face the nurse saw a plain answer in the affirmative.

"Yes," she said, "I see that's the trouble. Well, I know who took it."

"Then who was it?"

"Miss Garth!"

"Miss Garth! Nonsense!" cried Mr. Crellan, starting upright. "Nonsense!"

"It may be nonsense," the nurse replied slowly, with a monotonous emphasis on each word. "It may be nonsense, but it's a fact. I saw her take it."

Mr. Crellan simply gasped. Hewitt drew his chair a little nearer.

"If you saw her take it," he said gently, closely watching the woman's face the while, "then, of course, there's no doubt."

"I tell you I saw her take it," the nurse repeated. "What was in it, and what her game was in taking it, I don't know. But it was in that bureau, wasn't it?"

"Yes—probably."

"In the right hand top drawer?"

"Yes."

"A white paper in a blue envelope?"

"Yes."

"Then I saw her take it, as I said before. She unlocked that drawer before my eyes, took it out, and locked the drawer again."

Mr. Crellan turned blankly to Hewitt, but Hewitt kept his eyes on the nurse's face.

"When did this occur?" he asked, "and how?"

"It was on Saturday night, rather late. Everybody was in bed but Miss Garth and myself, and she had been down to the dining-room for something. Mr. Holford was asleep, so as I wanted to re-fill the water-bottle, I took it up and went. As I was passing the door of this room that we are in now, I heard a noise, and looked in at the door, which was open. There was a candle on the table which had been left there earlier in the evening. Miss Garth was opening the top right hand drawer of that bureau"—Mrs. Turton stabbed her finger spitefully toward the piece of furniture, as though she owed it a personal grudge— "and I saw her take out a blue foolscap envelope, and as the flap was open, I could see the enclosed paper was white. She shut the drawer, locked it, and came out of the room with the envelope in her hand."

"And what did you do?"

"I hurried on, and she came away without seeing me, and went in the opposite direction—toward the small staircase."

"Perhaps," Mr. Crellan ventured at a blurt, "perhaps she was walking in her sleep?"

"That she wasn't!" the nurse replied, "for she came back to Mr. Holford's room almost as soon as I returned there, and asked some questions about the medicine—which was nothing new, for I must say she was very fond of interfering in things that were part of my business."

"That is quite certain, I suppose," Hewitt remarked—"that she could not have been asleep?"

"Quite certain. She talked for about a quarter of an hour, and wanted to kiss Mr. Holford, which might have wakened him, before she went to bed. In fact, I may say we had a disagreement."

Hewitt did not take his steady gaze from the nurse's face for some seconds after she had finished speaking. Then he only said, "Thank you, Mrs. Turton. I need scarcely assure you, after what Mr. Crellan has said, that your confidence shall not be betrayed. I think that is all, unless you have more to tell us."

Mrs. Turton bowed and rose. "There is nothing more," she said, and left the room.

As soon as she had gone, "Is Mrs. Turton at all interested in the will," Hewitt asked.

"No, there is nothing for her. She is a newcomer, you see. Perhaps," Mr. Crellan went on, struck by an idea, "she may be jealous, or something. She seems a spiteful woman—and really, I can't believe her story for a moment."

"Why?"

"Well, you see, it's absurd. Why should Miss Garth go to all this secret trouble to do herself an injury—to make a beggar of herself? And besides, she's not in the habit of telling barefaced lies. She distinctly assured us, you remember, that she had never been to the bureau for any purpose whatever."

"But the nurse has an honest character, hasn't she?"

"Yes, her character is excellent. Indeed, from all accounts, she is a very excellent woman, except for a desire to govern everybody, and a habit of spite if she is thwarted. But, of course, that sort of thing sometimes leads people rather far."

"So it does," Hewitt replied. "But consider now. Is it not possible that Miss Garth, completely infatuated with Mr. Mellis, thinks she is doing a noble thing for him by destroying the will and giving up her whole claim to his uncle's property? Devoted women do just such things, you know."

Mr. Crellan stared, bent his head to his hand, and considered. "So they do, so they do," he said. "Insane foolery. Really, it's the sort of thing I can imagine her doing—she's honour and generosity itself. But then those lies," he resumed, sitting up and slapping his leg; "I can't believe she'd tell such tremendous lies as that for anybody. And with such a calm face, too—I'm sure she couldn't."

"Well, that's as it may be. You can scarcely set a limit to the lengths a woman will go on behalf of a man she loves. I suppose, by the bye, Miss Garth is not exactly what you would call a 'strong-minded' woman?"

"No, she's not that. She'd never get on in the world by herself. She's a good little soul, but nervous—very; and her month of anxiety, grief, and want of sleep seems to have broken her up."

"Mr. Mellis knows of the death, I suppose?"

"I telegraphed to him at his chambers in London the first thing yesterday—Tuesday—morning, as soon as the telegraph office was open. He came here (as I've forgotten to tell you as yet) the first thing this morning—before I was over here myself, in fact. He had been staying not far off—at Ockham, I think—and the telegram had been sent on. He saw Miss Garth, but couldn't stay, having to get back to London. I met him going away as I came, about eleven o'clock. Of course I said nothing about the fact that I couldn't find the will, but he will probably be down again soon, and may ask questions."

"Yes," Hewitt replied. "And speaking of that matter, you can no doubt talk with Miss Garth on very intimate and familiar terms?"

"Oh yes—yes; I've told you what old friends we are."

"I wish you could manage, at some favourable opportunity to-day, to speak to her alone, and without referring to the will in any way, get to know, as circumspectly and delicately as you can, how she stands in regard to Mr. Mellis. Whether he is an accepted lover, or likely to be one, you know. Whatever answer you may get, you may judge, I expect, by her manner how things really are."

"Very good—I'll seize the first chance. Meanwhile what to do?"

"Nothing, I'm afraid, except perhaps to examine other pieces of furniture as closely as we have examined this bureau."

Other bureaux, desks, tables, and chests were examined fruitlessly. It was not until after dinner that Mr. Crellan saw a favourable opportunity of sounding Miss Garth as he had promised. Half an hour later he came to Hewitt in the study, more puzzled than ever.

"There's no engagement between them,"'he reported, "secret or open, nor ever has been. It seems, from what I can make out, going to work as diplomatically as possible, that Mellis did propose to her, or something very near it, a time ago, and was point-blank refused. Altogether, Miss Garth's sentiment for him appears to be rather dislike than otherwise."

"That rather knocks a hole in the theory of self-sacrifice, doesn't it?" Hewitt remarked. "I shall have to think over this, and sleep on it. It's possible that it may be necessary to-morrow for you to tax Miss Garth, point-blank, with having taken away the will. Still, I hope not."

"I hope not, too," Mr. Crellan said, rather dubious as to the result of such an experiment. "She has been quite upset enough already. And, by the bye, she didn't seem any the better or more composed after Mellis' visit this morning."

"Still, then the will was gone."

"Yes."

And so Hewitt and Mr. Crellan talked on late into the evening, turning over every apparent possibility and finding reason in none. The household went to bed at ten, and, soon after, Miss Garth came to bid Mr. Crellan good-night. It had been settled that both Martin Hewitt and Mr. Crellan should stay the night at Wedbury Hall.

Soon all was still, and the ticking of the tall clock in the hall below could be heard as distinctly as though it were in the study, while the rain without dropped from eaves and sills in regular splashes. Twelve o'clock struck, and Mr. Crellan was about to suggest retirement, when the sound of a light footstep startled Hewitt's alert ear. He raised his hand to enjoin silence, and stepped to the door of the room, Mr. Crellan following him.

There was a light over the staircase, seven or eight yards away, and down the stairs came Miss Garth in dressing gown and slippers; she turned at the landing and vanished in a passage leading to the right.

"Where does that lead to?" Hewitt whispered hurriedly.

"Toward the small staircase—other end of house," Mr. Crellan replied in the same tones.

"Come quietly," said Hewitt, and stepped lightly after Miss Garth, Mr. Crellan at his heels.

She was nearing the opposite end of the passage, walking at a fair pace and looking neither to right nor left. There was another light over the smaller staircase at the end. Without hesitation Miss Garth turned down the stairs till about half down the flight, and then stopped and pressed her hand against the oak wainscot.

Immediately the vertical piece of framing against which she had placed her hand turned on central pivots top and bottom, revealing a small recess, three feet high and little more than six inches wide. Miss Garth stooped and felt about at the bottom of this recess for several seconds. Then with every sign of extreme agitation and horror she withdrew her hand empty, and sank on the stairs. Her head rolled from side to side on her shoulders, and beads of perspiration stood on her forehead. Hewitt with difficulty restrained Mr. Crellan from going to her assistance.

Presently, with a sort of shuddering sigh, Miss Garth rose, and after standing irresolute for a moment, descended the flight of stairs to the bottom. There she stopped again, and pressing her hand to her forehead, turned and began to re-ascend the stairs.

Hewitt touched his companion's arm, and the two hastily but noiselessly made their way back along the passage to the study. Miss Garth left the open framing as it was, reached the top of the landing, and without stopping proceeded along the passage and turned up the main staircase, while Hewitt and Mr. Crellan still watched her from the study door.

At the top of the flight she turned to the right, and up three or four more steps toward her own room. There she stopped, and leaned thoughtfully on the handrail.

"Go up," whispered Hewitt to Mr. Crellan, "as though you were going to bed. Appear surprised to see her; ask if she isn't well, and, if you can, manage to repeat that question of mine about secret hiding-places in the house."

Mr. Crellan nodded and started quickly up the stairs. Half-way up he turned his head, and, as he went on, "Why, Nelly, my dear," he said, "what's the matter? Aren't you well?"

Mr. Crellan acted his part well, and waiting below, Hewitt heard this dialogue:

"No, uncle, I don't feel very well, but it's nothing. I think my room seems close. I can scarcely breathe."

"Oh, it isn't close to-night. You'll be catching cold, my dear. Go and have a good sleep; you mustn't worry that wise little head of yours, you know. Mr. Hewitt and I have been making quite a night of it, but I'm off to bed now."

"I hope they've made you both quite comfortable, uncle?"

"Oh, yes; capital, capital. We've been talking over business, and, no doubt, we shall put that matter all in order soon. By the bye, I suppose since you saw Mr. Hewitt you haven't happened to remember anything more to tell him?"

"No."

"You still can't remember any hiding-places or panels, or that sort of thing in the wainscot or anywhere?"

"No, I'm sure I don't know of any, and I don't believe for a moment that any exist."

"Quite sure of that, I suppose?"

"Oh yes."

"All right. Now go to bed. You'll catch such a cold in these draughty landings. Come, I won't move a step till I see your door shut behind you. Good-night."

"Good-night, uncle."

Mr. Crellan came downstairs again with a face of blank puzzlement.

"I wouldn't have believed it," he assured Martin Hewitt; "positively I wouldn't have believed she'd have told such a lie, and with such confidence, too. There's something deep and horrible here, I'm afraid. What does it mean?"

"We'll talk of that afterwards," Hewitt replied. "Come now and take a look at that recess."

They went, quietly still, to the small staircase and there, with a candle, closely examined the recess. It was a mere box, three feet high, a foot or a little more deep, and six or seven inches wide. The piece of oak framing, pivoted to the stair at the bottom and to a horizontal piece of framing at the top, stood edge forward, dividing the opening down the centre. There was nothing whatever in the recess.

Hewitt ascertained that there was no catch, the plank simply remaining shut by virtue of fitting tightly, so that nothing but pressure on the proper part was requisite to open it. He had closed the plank and turned to speak to Mr. Crellan, when another interruption occurred.

On each floor the two staircases were joined by passages, and the ground-floor passage, from the foot of the flight they were on, led to the entrance hall. Distinct amid the loud clicking of the hall clock, Hewitt now heard a sound, as of a person's foot shifting on a stone step.

Mr. Crellan heard it too, and each glanced at the other. Then Hewitt, shading the candle with his hand, led the way to the hall. There they listened for several seconds—almost an hour—it seemed—and then the noise was repeated. There was no doubt of it. It was at the other side of the front door.

In answer to Hewitt's hurried whispers, Mr. Crellan assured him that there was no window from which, in the dark, a view could be got of a person standing outside the door. Also that any other way out would be equally noisy, and would entail the circuit of the house. The front door was fastened by three heavy bolts, an immense old-fashioned lock, and a bar. It would take nearly a minute to open at least, even if everything went easily. But, as there was no other way, Hewitt determined to try it. Handing the candle to his companion, he first lifted the bar, conceiving that it might be done with the least noise. It went easily, and, handling it carefully, Hewitt let it hang from its rivet without a sound. Just then, glancing at Mr. Crellan, he saw that he was forgetting to shade the candle, whose rays extended through the fanlight above the door, and probably through the wide crack under it. But it was too late. At the same moment the light was evidently perceived from outside; there was a hurried jump from the steps, and for an instant a sound of running on gravel. Hewitt tore back the bolts, flung the door open, and dashed out into the darkness, leaving Mr. Crellan on the doorstep with the candle.

Hewitt was gone, perhaps, five or ten minutes, although to Mr. Crellan—standing there at the open door in a state of high nervous tension, and with no notion of what was happening or what it all meant—the time seemed an eternity. When at last Hewitt reached the door again, "What was it?" asked Mr. Crellan, much agitated. "Did you see? Have you caught them?"

Hewitt shook his head.

"I hadn't a chance," he said. "The wall is low over there, and there's a plantation of trees at the other side. But I think—yes, I begin to think—that I may possibly be able to see my way through this business in a little while. See this?"

On the top step in the sheltered porch there remained the wet prints of two feet. Hewitt took a letter from his pocket, opened it out, spread it carefully over the more perfect of the two marks, pressed it lightly and lifted it. Then, when the door was shut, he produced his pocket scissors, and with great care cut away the paper round the wet part, leaving a piece, of course, the shape of a boot sole.

"Come," said Hewitt, "we may get at something after all. Don't ask me to tell you anything now; I don't know anything, as a matter of fact. I hope this is the end of the night's entertainment, but I'm afraid the case is rather an unpleasant business. There is nothing for us to do now but to go to bed, I think. I suppose there's a handy man kept about the place?"

"Yes, he's gardener and carpenter and carpetbeater, and so on."

"Good! Where's his sanctum? Where does he keep his shovels and carpet sticks?"

"In the shed by the coach house, I believe. I think it's generally unlocked."

"Very good. We've earned a night's rest, and now we'll have it."

The next morning, after breakfast, Hewitt took Mr. Crellan into the study.

"Can you manage," he said, "to send Miss Garth out for a walk this morning—with somebody?"

"I can send her out for a ride with the groom—unless she thinks it wouldn't be the thing to go riding so soon after her bereavement."

"Never mind, that will do. Send her at once, and see that she goes. Call it doctor's orders; say she must go for her health's sake—anything."

Mr. Crellan departed, used his influence, and in half an hour Miss Garth had gone.

"I was up pretty early this morning," Hewitt remarked on Mr. Crellan's return to the study, "and, among other things, I sent a telegram to London. Unless my eyes deceive me, a boy with a peaked cap—a telegraph boy, in fact—is coming up the drive this moment. Yes, he is. It is probably my answer."

In a few minutes a telegram was brought in. Hewitt read it and then asked,—

"Your friend Mr. Mellis, I understand, was going straight to town yesterday morning?"

"Yes."

"Read that, then."

Mr. Crellan took the telegram and read:

"MELLIS DID NOT SLEEP AT CHAMBERS LAST NIGHT. BEEN OUT OF TOWN FOR SOME DAYS PAST. KERRETT."

Mr. Crellan looked up.

"Who's Kerrett?" he asked.

"Lad in my office; sharp fellow. You see, Mellis didn't go to town after all. As a matter of fact, I believe he was nearer this place than we thought. You said he had a disagreement with his uncle because of scientific practices which the old gentleman considered 'dangerous and unprofessional,' I think?"

"Yes, that was the case."

"Ah, then the key to all the mystery of the will is in this room."

"Where?"

"There." Hewitt pointed to the book-cases. "Read Bernheim's Suggestive Therapeutics, and one or two books of Heidenhain's and Bjornstrom's and you'll see the thing more clearly than you can without them; but that would be rather a long sort of job, so—but why, who's this? Somebody coming up the drive in a fly, isn't it?"

"Yes," Mr. Crellan replied, looking out of the window. Presently he added, "It's Cranley Mellis."

"Ah," said Hewitt, "he won't trouble us for a little. I'll bet you a penny cake he goes first by himself to the small staircase and tries that secret recess. If you get a little way along the passage you will be able to see him; but that will scarcely matter—I can see you don't guess now what I am driving at."

"I don't in the least."

"I told you the names of the books in which you could read the matter up; but that would be too long for the present purpose. The thing is fairly well summarised, I see, in that encyclopaedia there in the corner. I have put a marker in volume seven. Do you mind opening it at that place and seeing for yourself?"

Mr. Crellan, doubtful and bewildered, reached the volume. It opened readily, and in the place where it opened lay a blue foolscap envelope. The old gentleman took the envelope, drew from it a white paper, stared first at the paper, then at Hewitt, then at the paper again, let the volume slide from his lap, and gasped,—

"Why—why—it's the will!"

"Ah, so I thought," said Hewitt, catching the book as it fell. "But don't lose this place in the encyclopaedia. Read the name of the article. What is it?"

Mr. Crellan looked absent-mindedly at the title, holding the will before him all the time. Then, mechanically, he read aloud the word, "Hypnotism."

"Hypnotism it is," Hewitt answered. "A dangerous and terrible power in the hands of an unscrupulous man."

"But—but how? I don't understand it. This—this is the real will, I suppose?"

"Look at it; you know best."

Mr. Crellan looked.

"Yes," he said, "this certainly is the will. But where did it come from? It hasn't been in this book all the time, has it?"

"No. Didn't I tell you I put it there myself as a marker? But come, you'll understand my explanation better if I first read you a few lines from this article. See here now:—

"'Although hypnotism has power for good when properly used by medical men, it is an exceedingly dangerous weapon in the hands of the unskilful or unscrupulous. Crimes have been committed by persons who have been hypnotised. Just as a person when hypnotised is rendered extremely impressionable, and therefore capable of receiving beneficial suggestions, so he is nearly as liable to receive suggestions for evil; and it is quite possible for an hypnotic subject, while under hypnotic influence, to be impressed with the belief that he is to commit some act after the influence is removed, and that act he is safe to commit, acting at the time as an automaton. Suggestions may be thus made of which the subject, in his subsequent uninfluenced moments, has no idea, but which he will proceed to carry out automatically at the time appointed. In the case of a complete state of hypnotism the subject has subsequently no recollection whatever of what has happened. Persons whose will or nerve power has been weakened by fear or other similar causes can be hypnotised without consent on their part.'

"There now, what do you make of that?"

"Why, do you mean that Miss Garth has been hypnotised by—by—Cranley Mellis?"

"I think that is the case; indeed, I am pretty sure of it. Notice, on the occasion of each of his last two visits, he was alone with Miss Garth for some little time. On the evening following each of those visits she does something which she afterwards knows nothing about—something connected with the disappearance of this will, the only thing standing between Mr. Mellis and the whole of his uncle's property. Who could have been in a weaker nervous state than Miss Garth has been lately? Remember, too, on the visit of last Saturday, while Miss Garth says she only showed Mellis to the door, both you and the nurse speak of their being gone some little time. Miss Garth must have forgotten what took place then, when Mellis hypnotised her, and impressed on her the suggestion that she should take Mr. Holford's will that night, long after he—Mellis—had gone, and when he could not be suspected of knowing anything of it. Further, that she should, at that time when her movements would be less likely to be observed, secrete that will in a place of hiding known only to himself."

"Dear, dear, what a rascal! Do you really think he did that?"

"Not only that, but I believe he came here yesterday morning while you were out to get the will from the recess. The recess, by the bye, I expect he discovered by accident on one of his visits (he has been here pretty often, I suppose, altogether), and kept the secret in case it might be useful. Yesterday, not finding the will there, he hypnotised Miss Garth once again, and conveyed the suggestion that, at midnight last night, she should take the will from wherever she had put it and pass it to him under the front door."

"What, do you mean it was he you chased across the grounds last night?"

"That is a thing I am pretty certain of. If we had Mr. Mellis's boot here we could make sure by comparing it with the piece of paper I cut out, as you will remember, in the entrance hall. As we have the will, though, that will scarcely be necessary. What he will do now, I expect, will be to go to the recess again on the vague chance of the will being there now, after all, assuming that his second dose of mesmerism has somehow miscarried. If Miss Garth were here he might try his tricks again, and that is why I got you to send her out."

"And where did you find the will?"

"Now you come to practical details. You will remember that I asked about the handyman's toolhouse? Well, I paid it a visit at six o'clock this morning, and found therein some very excellent carpenter's tools in a chest. I took a selection of them to the small staircase, and took out the tread of a stair—the one that the pivoted framing-plank rested on."

"And you found the will there?"

"The will, as I rather expected when I examined the recess last night, had slipped down a rather wide crack at the end of the stair timber, which, you know, formed, so to speak, the floor of the recess. The fact was, the stair-tread didn't quite reach as far as the back of the recess. The opening wasn't very distinct to see, but I soon felt it with my fingers. When Miss Garth, in her hypnotic condition on Saturday night, dropped the will into the recess, it shot straight to the back corner and fell down the slit. That was why Mellis found it empty, and why Miss Garth also found it empty on returning there last night under hypnotic influence. You observed her terrible state of nervous agitation when she failed to carry out the command that haunted her. It was frightful. Something like what happens to a suddenly awakened somnambulist, perhaps. Anyway, that is all over. I found the will under the end of the stair-tread, and here it is. If you will come to the small staircase now you shall see where the paper slipped out of sight. Perhaps we shall meet Mr. Mellis."

"He's a scoundrel," said Mr. Crellan. "It's a pity we can't punish him."

"That's impossible, of course. Where's your proof? And if you had any I'm not sure that a hypnotist is responsible at law for what his subject does. Even if he were, moving a will from one part of the house to another is scarcely a legal crime. The explanation I have given you accounts entirely for the disturbed manner of Miss Garth in the presence of Mellis. She merely felt an indefinite sense of his power over her. Indeed, there is all the possibility that, finding her an easy subject, he had already practised his influence by way of experiment. A hypnotist, as you will see in the books, has always an easier task with a person he has hypnotised before."

As Hewitt had guessed, in the corridor they met Mr. Mellis. He was a thin, dark man of about thirty-five, with large, bony features, and a slight stoop. Mr. Crellan glared at him ferociously.

"Well, sir, and what do you want?" he asked.

Mr. Mellis looked surprised. "Really, that's a very extraordinary remark, Mr. Crellan," he said. "This is my late uncle's house. I might, with at least as much reason, ask you what you want."

"I'm here, sir, as Mr. Holford's executor."

"Appointed by will?"

"Yes."

"And is the will in existence?"

"Well—the fact is—we couldn't find it—"

"Then, what do you mean, sir, by calling yourself an executor with no will to warrant you?" interrupted Mellis. "Get out of this house. If there's no will, I administrate."

"But there is a will," roared Mr. Crellan, shaking it in his face. "There is a will. I didn't say we hadn't found it yet, did I? There is a will, and here it is in spite of all your diabolical tricks, with your scoundrelly hypnotism and secret holes, and the rest of it! Get out of this place, sir, or I'll have you thrown out of the window!"

Mr. Mellis shrugged his shoulders with an appearance of perfect indifference. "If you've a will appointing you executor it's all right, I suppose, although I shall take care to hold you responsible for any irregularities. As I don't in the least understand your conduct, unless it is due to drink, I'll leave you." And with that he went.

Mr. Crellan boiled with indignation for a minute, and then turning to Hewitt, "I say, I hope it's all right," he said, "connecting him with all this queer business?"

"We shall soon see," replied Hewitt, "if you'll come and look at the pivoted plank."

They went to the small staircase, and Hewitt once again opened the recess. Within lay a blue foolscap envelope, which Hewitt picked up. "See," he said, "it is torn at the corner. He has been here and opened it. It's a fresh envelope, and I left it for him this morning, with the corner gummed down a little so that he would have to tear it in opening. This is what was inside," Hewitt added, and laughed aloud as he drew forth a rather crumpled piece of white paper. "It was only a childish trick after all," he concluded, "but I always liked a small practical joke on occasion." He held out the crumpled paper, on which was inscribed in large capital letters the single word—"SOLD."

IV. — THE CASE OF THE MISSING HAND

I think I have recorded in another place Hewitt's frequent aphorism that "there is nothing in this world that is at all possible that has not happened or is not happening in London." But there are many strange happenings in this matter-of-fact country and in these matter-of-fact times that occur far enough from London. Fantastic crimes, savage revenges, mediaeval superstitions, horrible cruelty, though less in sight, have been no more extinguished by the advent of the nineteenth century than have the ancient races who practised them in the dark ages. Some of the races have become civilized, and some of the savageries are heard of no more. But there are survivals in both cases. I say these things having in my mind a particular case that came under the personal notice of both Hewitt and myself—an affair that brought one up standing with a gasp and a doubt of one's era.

My good uncle, the Colonel, was not in the habit of gathering large house parties at his place at Ratherby, partly because the place was not a great one, and partly because the Colonel's gout was. But there was an excellent bit of shooting for two or three guns, and even when he was unable to leave the house himself, my uncle was always pleased if some good friend were enjoying a good day's sport in his territory. As to myself, the good old soul was in a perpetual state of offence because I visited him so seldom, though whenever my scant holidays fell in a convenient time of the year I was never insensible to the attractions of the Ratherby stubble. More than once had I sat by the old gentleman when his foot was exceptionally troublesome, amusing him with accounts of some of the doings of Martin Hewitt, and more than once had my uncle expressed his desire to meet Hewitt himself, and commissioned me with an invitation to be presented to Hewitt at the first likely opportunity, for a joint excursion to Ratherby. At length I persuaded Hewitt to take a fortnight's rest, coincident with a little vacation of my own, and we got down to Ratherby within a few days past September the 1st, and before a gun had been fired at the Colonel's bit of shooting. The Colonel himself we found confined to the house with his foot on the familiar rest, and though ourselves were the only guests, we managed to do pretty well together. It was during this short holiday that the case I have mentioned arose.

When first I began to record some of the more interesting of Hewitt's operations, I think I explained that such cases as I myself had not witnessed I should set down in impersonal narrative form, without intruding myself. The present case, so far as Hewitt's work was concerned, I saw, but there were circumstances which led up to it that we only fully learned afterwards. These circumstances, however, I shall put in their proper place—at the beginning.

The Fosters were a fairly old Ratherby family, of whom Mr. John Foster had died by an accident at the age of about forty, leaving a wife twelve years younger than himself and three children, two boys and one girl, who was the youngest. The boys grew up strong, healthy, out-of-door young ruffians, with all the tastes of sportsmen, and all the qualities, good and bad, natural to lads of fairly well-disposed character allowed a great deal too much of their own way from the beginning.

Their only real bad quality was an unfortunate knack of bearing malice, and a certain savage vindictiveness towards such persons as they chose to consider their enemies. With the louts of the village they were at unceasing war, and, indeed, once got into serious trouble for peppering the butcher's son (who certainly was a great blackguard) with sparrow-shot. At the usual time they went to Oxford together, and were fraternally sent down together in their second year, after enjoying a spell of rustication in their first. The offence was never specifically mentioned about Ratherby, but was rumoured of as something particularly outrageous.

It was at this time, sixteen years or thereabout after the death of their father, that Henry and Robert Foster first saw and disliked Mr. Jonas Sneathy, a director of penny banks and small insurance offices. He visited Ranworth (the Fosters' home) a great deal more than the brothers thought necessary, and, indeed, it was not for lack of rudeness on their part that Mr. Sneathy failed to understand, as far as they were concerned, his room was preferred to his company.

But their mother welcomed him, and in the end it was announced that Mrs. Foster was to marry again, and that after that her name would be Mrs. Sneathy.

Hereupon there were violent scenes at Ranworth. Henry and Robert Foster denounced their prospective father-in-law as a fortune-hunter, a snuffler, a hypocrite. They did not stop at broad hints as to the honesty of his penny banks and insurance offices, and the house straightway became a house of bitter strife. The marriage took place, and it was not long before Mr. Sneathy's real character became generally obvious. For months he was a model, if somewhat sanctimonious husband, and his influence over his wife was complete. Then he discovered that her property had been strictly secured by her first husband's will, and that, willing as she might be, she was unable to raise money for her new husband's benefit, and was quite powerless to pass to him any of her property by deed of gift. Hereupon the man's nature showed itself. Foolish woman as Mrs. Sneathy might be, she was a loving, indeed, an infatuated wife; but Sneathy repaid her devotion by vulgar derision, never hesitating to state plainly that he had married her for his own profit, and that he considered himself swindled in the result. More, he even proceeded to blows and other practical brutality of a sort only devisable by a mean and ugly nature. This treatment, at first secret, became open, and in the midst of it Mr. Sneathy's penny banks and insurance offices came to a grievous smash all at once, and everybody wondered how Mr. Sneathy kept out of gaol.

Keep out of gaol he did, however, for he had taken care to remain on the safe side of the law, though some of his co-directors learnt the taste of penal servitude. But he was beggared, and lived, as it were, a mere pensioner in his wife's house. Here his brutality increased to a frightful extent, till his wife, already broken in health in consequence, went in constant fear of her life, and Miss Foster passed a life of weeping misery. All her friends' entreaties, however, could not persuade Mrs. Sneathy to obtain a legal separation from her husband. She clung to him with the excuse—for it was no more—that she hoped to win him to kindness by submission, and with a pathetic infatuation that seemed to increase as her bodily strength diminished.

Henry and Robert, as may be supposed, were anything but silent in these circumstances. Indeed, they broke out violently again and again, and more than once went near permanently injuring their worthy father-in-law. Once especially, when Sneathy, absolutely without provocation, made a motion to strike his wife in their presence, there was a fearful scene. The two sprang at him like wild beasts, knocked him down and dragged him to the balcony with the intention of throwing him out of the window. But Mrs. Sneathy impeded them, hysterically imploring them to desist.

"If you lift your hand to my mother," roared Henry, gripping Sneathy by the throat till his fat face turned blue, and banging his head against the wall, "if you lift your hand to my mother again I'll chop it off—I will! I'll chop it off and drive it down your throat!"

"We'll do worse," said Robert, white and frantic with passion, "we'll hang you—hang you to the door! You're a proved liar and thief, and you're worse than a common murderer. I'd hang you to the front door for twopence!"

For a few days Sneathy was comparatively quiet, cowed by their violence. Then he took to venting redoubled spite on his unfortunate wife, always in the absence of her sons, well aware that she would never inform them. On their part, finding him apparently better behaved in consequence of their attack, they thought to maintain his wholesome terror, and scarcely passed him without a menace, taking a fiendish delight in repeating the threats they had used during the scene, by way of keeping it present to his mind.

"Take care of your hands, sir," they would say. "Keep them to yourself, or, by George, we'll take 'em off with a billhook!"

But his revenge for all this Sneathy took unobserved on their mother. Truly a miserable household.

Soon, however, the brothers left home, and went to London by way of looking for a profession. Henry began a belated study of medicine, and Robert made a pretence of reading for the bar. Indeed, their departure was as much as anything a consequence of the earnest entreaty of their sister, who saw that their presence at home was an exasperation to Sneathy, and aggravated her mother's secret sufferings. They went, therefore; but at Ranworth things became worse.

Little was allowed to be known outside the house, but it was broadly said that Mr. Sneathy's behaviour had now become outrageous beyond description. Servants left faster than new ones could be found, and gave their late employer the character of a raving maniac. Once, indeed, he committed himself in the village, attacking with his walking-stick an inoffensive tradesman who had accidentally brushed against him, and immediately running home. This assault had to be compounded for by a payment of fifty pounds. And then Henry and Robert Foster received a most urgent letter from their sister requesting their immediate presence at home.

They went at once, of course, and the servants' account of what occurred was this. When the brothers arrived Mr. Sneathy had just left the house. The brothers were shut up with their mother and sister for about a quarter of an hour, and then left them and came out to the stable yard together. The coachman (he was a new man, who had only arrived the day before) overheard a little of their talk as they stood by the door.

Mr. Henry said that "the thing must be done, and at once. There are two of us, so that it ought to be easy enough." And afterwards Mr. Robert said, "You'll know best how to go about it, as a doctor." After which Mr. Henry came towards the coachman and asked in what direction Mr. Sneathy had gone. The coachman replied that it was in the direction of Ratherby Wood, by the winding footpath that led through it. But as he spoke he distinctly with the corner of his eye saw the other brother take a halter from a hook by the stable door and put it into his coat pocket.

So far for the earlier events, whereof I learned later bit by bit. It was on the day of the arrival of the brothers Foster at their old home, and, indeed, little more than two hours after the incident last set down, that news of Mr. Sneathy came to Colonel Brett's place, where Hewitt and I were sitting and chatting with the Colonel. The news was that Mr. Sneathy had committed suicide—had been found hanging, in fact, to a tree in Ratherby Wood, just by the side of the footpath.

Hewitt and I had of course at this time never heard of Sneathy, and the Colonel told us what little he knew. He had never spoken to the man, he said—indeed, nobody in the place outside Ranworth would have anything to do with him. "He's certainly been an unholy scoundrel over those poor people's banks," said my uncle, "and if what they say's true, he's been about as bad as possible to his wretched wife. He must have been pretty miserable, too, with all his scoundrelism, for he was a completely ruined man, without a chance of retrieving his position, and detested by everybody. Indeed, some of his recent doings, if what I have heard is to be relied on, have been very much those of a madman. So that, on the whole, I'm not much surprised. Suicide's about the only crime, I suppose, that he has never experimented with till now, and, indeed, it's rather a service to the world at large—his only service, I expect."

The Colonel sent a man to make further inquiries, and presently this man returned with the news that now it was said that Mr. Sneathy had not committed suicide, but had been murdered. And hard on the man's heels came Mr. Hardwick, a neighbour of my uncle's and a fellow J. P. He had had the case reported to him, it seemed, as soon as the body had been found, and had at once gone to the spot. He had found the body hanging—and with the right hand cut off.

"It's a murder, Brett," he said, "without doubt—a most horrible case of murder and mutilation. The hand is cut off and taken away, but whether the atrocity was committed before or after the hanging of course

I can't say. But the missing hand makes it plainly a case of murder, and not suicide. I've come to consult you about issuing a warrant, for I think there's no doubt as to the identity of the murderers."

"That's a good job," said the Colonel, "else we should have had some work for Mr. Martin' Hewitt here, which wouldn't be fair, as he's taking a rest. Whom do you think of having arrested?"

"The two young Fosters. It's plain as it can be—and a most revolting crime too, bad as Sneathy may have been. They came down from London to-day and went out deliberately to it, it's clear. They were heard talking of it, asked as to the direction in which he had gone, and followed him—and with a rope."

"Isn't that rather an unusual form of murder—hanging?" Hewitt remarked.

"Perhaps it is," Mr. Hardwick replied; "but it's the case here plain enough. It seems, in fact, that they had a way of threatening to hang him and even to cut off his hand if he used it to strike their mother. So that they appear to have carried out what might have seemed mere idle threats in a diabolically savage way. Of course they may have strangled him first and hanged him after, by way of carrying out their threat and venting their spite on the mutilated body. But that they did it is plain enough for me. I've spent an hour or two over it, and feel I am certainly more than justified in ordering their apprehension. Indeed, they were with him at the time, as I have found by their tracks on the footpath through the wood."

The Colonel turned to Martin Hewitt. "Mr. Hardwick, you must know," he said, "is by way of being an amateur in your particular line—and a very good amateur, too, I should say, judging by a case or two I have known in this county."

Hewitt bowed, and laughingly expressed a fear lest Mr. Hardwick should come to London and supplant him altogether. "This seems a curious case," he added. "If you don't mind, I think I should like to take a glance at the tracks and whatever other traces there may be, just by way of keeping my hand in."

"Certainly," Mr. Hardwick replied, brightening. "I should of all things like to have Mr. Hewitt's opinions on the observations I have made—just for my own gratification. As to his opinion—there can be no room for doubt; the thing is plain."

With many promises not to be late for dinner, we left my uncle and walked with Mr. Hardwick in the direction of Ratherby Wood. It was an unfrequented part, he told us, and by particular care he had managed, he hoped, to prevent the rumour spreading to the village yet, so that we might hope to find the trails not yet overlaid. It was a man of his own, he said, who, making a short cut through the wood, had come upon the body hanging, and had run immediately to inform him. With this man he had gone back, cut down the body, and made his observations. He had followed the trail backward to Ranworth, and there had found the new coachman, who had once been in his own service. From him he had learned the doings of the brothers Foster as they left the place, and from him he had ascertained that they had not then returned. Then, leaving his man by the body, he had come straight to my uncle's.

Presently we came on the footpath leading from Ranworth across the field to Ratherby Wood. It was a mere trail of bare earth worn by successive feet amid the grass. It was damp, and we all stooped and examined the footmarks that were to be seen on it. They all pointed one way—towards the wood in the distance.

"Fortunately it's not a greatly frequented path," Mr. Hardwick—said. "You see, there are the marks of three pairs of feet only, and as first Sneathy and then both of the brothers came this way, these footmarks must be theirs. Which are Sneathy's is plain—they are these large flat ones. If you notice, they are all distinctly visible in the centre of the track, showing plainly that they belong to the man who walked alone, which was Sneathy. Of the others, the marks of the outside feet—the left on the left side and the right on the right—are often not visible. Clearly they belong to two men walking side by side, and more often than not treading, with their outer feet, on the grass at the side. And where these happen to drop on the same spot as the marks in the middle they cover them. Plainly they are the footmarks of Henry and Robert Foster, made as they followed Sneathy. Don't you agree with me Mr. Hewitt?"

"Oh yes, that's very plain. You have a better pair of eyes than most people, Mr. Hardwick, and a good idea of using them, too. We will go into the wood now. As a matter of fact I can pretty clearly distinguish most of the other foot-marks—those on the grass; but that's a matter of much training."

We followed the footpath, keeping on the grass at its side, in case it should be desirable to refer again to the foot-tracks. For some little distance into the wood the tracks continued as before, those of the brothers overlaying those of Sneathy. Then there was a difference. The path here was broader and muddy, because of the proximity of trees, and suddenly the outer footprints separated, and no more overlay the larger ones in the centre, but proceeded at an equal distance on either side of them.

"See there!" cried Mr. Hardwick, pointing triumphantly to the spot, "this is where they overtook him, and walked on either side. The body was found only a little farther on—you could see the place now if the path didn't zigzag about so."

Hewitt said nothing, but stooped and examined the tracks at the sides with great care and evident thought, spanning the distances between them comparatively with his arms. Then he rose and stepped lightly from one mark to another, taking care not to tread on the mark itself. "Very good," he said shortly on finishing his examination. "We'll go on."

We went on, and presently came to the place where the body lay. Here the ground sloped from the left down towards the right, and a tiny streamlet, a mere trickle of a foot or two wide, ran across the path. In rainy seasons it was probably wider, for all the earth and clay had been washed away for some feet on each side, leaving flat, bare and very coarse gravel, on which the trail was lost. Just beyond this, and to the left, the body lay on a grassy knoll under the limb of a tree, from which still depended a part of the cut rope. It was not a pleasant sight. The man was a soft, fleshy creature, probably rather under than over the medium height, and he lay there, with his stretched neck and protruding tongue, a revolting object. His right arm lay by his side, and the stump of the wrist was clotted with black blood. Mr. Hardwick's man was still in charge, seemingly little pleased with his job, and a few yards off stood a couple of countrymen looking on.

Hewitt asked from which direction these men had come, and having ascertained and noticed their footmarks, he asked them to stay exactly where they were, to avoid confusing such other tracks as might be seen. Then he addressed himself to his examination. "First," he said, glancing up at the branch, that was scarce a yard above his head, "this rope has been here for some time."

"Yes," Mr. Hardwick replied, "it's an old swing rope. Some children used it in the summer, but it got partly cut away, and the odd couple of yards has been hanging since."

"Ah," said Hewitt, "then if the Fosters did this they were saved some trouble by the chance, and were able to take their halter back with them—and so avoid one chance of detection." He very closely scrutinised the top of a tree stump, probably the relic of a tree that had been cut down long before, and then addressed himself to the body.

"When you cut it down," he said, "did it fall in a heap?"

"No, my man eased it down to some extent."

"Not on to its face?"

"Oh no. On to its back, just as it is now." Mr Hardwick saw that Hewitt was looking at muddy marks on each of the corpse's knees, to one of which a small leaf clung, and at one or two other marks of the same sort on the fore part of the dress. "That seems to show pretty plainly," he said, "that he must have struggled with them and was thrown forward, doesn't it?"

Hewitt did not reply, but gingerly lifted the right arm by its sleeve. "Is either of the brothers Foster left-handed?" he asked.

"No, I think not. Here, Bennett, you have seen plenty of their doings—cricket, shooting, and so on—do you remember if either is left-handed?"

"Nayther, sir," Mr. Hardwick's man answered. "Both on 'em's right-handed."

Hewitt lifted the lapel of the coat and attentively regarded a small rent in it. The dead man's hat lay near, and after a few glances at that, Hewitt dropped it and turned his attention to the hair. This was coarse and dark and long, and brushed straight back with no parting.

"This doesn't look very symmetrical, does it?" Hewitt remarked, pointing to the locks over the right ear. They were shorter just there than on the other side, and apparently very clumsily cut, whereas in every other part the hair appeared to be rather well and carefully trimmed. Mr. Hardwick said nothing, but fidgeted a little, as though he considered that valuable time was being wasted over irrelevant trivialities.

Presently, however, he spoke. "There's very little to be learned from the body, is there?" he said. "I think I'm quite justified in ordering their arrest, eh?—indeed, I've wasted too much time already."

Hewitt was groping about among some bushes behind the tree from which the corpse had been taken. When he answered, he said, "I don't think I should do anything of the sort just now, Mr. Hardwick. As a matter of fact, I fancy"—this word with an emphasis—"that the brothers Foster may not have seen this man Sneathy at all to-day."

"Not seen him? Why, my dear sir, there's no question of it. It's certain, absolutely. The evidence is positive. The fact of the threats and of the body being found treated so is pretty well enough, I should think. But that's nothing—look at those footmarks. They've walked along with him, one each side, without a possible doubt; plainly they were the last people with him, in any case. And you don't mean to ask anybody to believe that the dead man, even if he hanged himself, cut off his own hand first. Even if you do, where's the hand? And even putting aside all these considerations, each a complete case in itself, the Fosters must at least have seen the body as they came past, and yet nothing has been heard of them yet.

"Why didn't they spread the alarm? They went Straight away in the opposite direction from home—there are their footmarks, which you've not seen yet, beyond the gravel."

Hewitt stepped over to where the patch of clean gravel ceased, at the opposite side to that from which we had approached the brook, and there, sure enough, were the now familiar footmarks of the brothers leading away from the scene of Sneathy's end. "Yes," Hewitt said, "I see them. Of course, Mr. Hardwick, you'll do what seems right in your own eyes, and in any case not much harm will be done by the arrest beyond a terrible fright for that unfortunate family. Nevertheless, if you care for my impression, it is, as I have said, that the Fosters have not seen Sneathy to-day."

"But what about the hand?"

"As to that I have a conjecture, but as yet it is only a conjecture, and if I told it you would probably call it absurd—certainly you'd disregard it, and perhaps quite excusably. The case is a complicated one, and, if there is anything at all in my conjecture, one of the most remarkable I have ever had to do with. It interests me intensely, and I shall devote a little time now to following up the theory I have formed. You have, I suppose, already communicated with the police?"

"I wired to Shopperton at once, as soon as I heard of the matter. It's a twelve miles drive, but I wonder the police have not arrived yet. They can't be long; I don't know where the village constable has got to, but in any case he wouldn't be much good. But as to your idea that the Fosters can't be suspected—well, nobody could respect your opinion, Mr. Hewitt, more than myself, but really, just think. The notion's impossible—fifty-fold impossible. As soon as the police arrive I shall have that trail followed and the Fosters apprehended. I should be a fool if I didn't."

"Very well, Mr. Hardwick," Hewitt replied; "you'll do what you consider your duty, of course, and quite properly, though I would recommend you to take another glance at those three trails in the path. I shall take a look in this direction." And he turned up by the side of the streamlet, keeping on the gravel at its side.

I followed. We climbed the rising ground, and presently, among the trees, came to the place where the little rill emerged from the broken ground in the highest part of the wood. Here the clean ground ceased, and there was a large patch of wet clayey earth. Several marks left by the feet of cattle were there, and one or two human footmarks. Two of these (a pair), the newest and the most distinct, Hewitt studied carefully, and measured each direction.

"Notice these marks," he said. "They may be of importance or they may not—that we shall see. Fortunately they are very distinctive—the right boot is a badly worn one, and a small tag of leather, where the soul is damaged, is doubled over and trodden into the soft earth. Nothing could be luckier. Clearly they are the most recent footsteps in this direction—from the main road, which lies right ahead, through the rest of the wood."

"Then you think somebody else has been on the scene of the tragedy, beside the victim and the brothers?" I said.

"Yes, I do. But hark; there is a vehicle in the road. Can you see between the trees? Yes, it is the police cart. We shall be able to report its arrival to Mr. Hardwick as we go down."

We turned and walked rapidly down the incline to where we had come from. Mr. Hardwick and his man were still there, and another rustic had arrived to gape. We told Mr. Hardwick that he might expect the police presently, and proceeded along the gravel skirting the stream, toward the lower part of the wood.

Here Hewitt proceeded very cautiously, keeping a sharp look-out on either side for footprints on the neighbouring soft ground. There were none, however, for the gravel margin of the stream made a sort of footpath of itself, and the trees and undergrowth were close and thick on each side. At the bottom we emerged from the wood on a small piece of open ground skirting a lane, and here, just by the side of the lane, where the stream fell into a trench, Hewitt suddenly pounced on another footmark. He was unusually excited.

"See," he said, "here it is—the right foot with its broken leather, and the corresponding left foot on the damp edge of the lane itself. He—the man with the broken shoe—has walked on the hard gravel all the way down from the source of the stream, and his is the only trail unaccounted for near the body. Come, Brett, we've an adventure on foot. Do you care to let your uncle's dinner go by the board, and follow?"

"Can't we go back and tell him?"

"No—there's no time to lose; we must follow up this man—or at least I must. You go or stay, of course, as you think best."

I hesitated a moment, picturing to myself the excellent Colonel as he would appear after waiting dinner an hour or two for us, but decided to go. "At any rate," I said, "if the way lies along the roads we shall probably meet somebody going in the direction of Ratherby who will take a message. But what is your theory? I don't understand at all. I must say everything Hardwick said seemed to me to be beyond question. There were the tracks to prove that the three had walked together to the spot, and that the brothers had gone on alone; and every other circumstance pointed the same way. Then, what possible motive could anybody else about here have for such a crime? Unless, indeed, it were one of the people defrauded by Sneathy's late companies."

"The motive," said Hewitt, "is, I fancy, a most extraordinary—indeed, a weird one. A thing as of centuries ago. Ask me no questions—I think you will be a little surprised before very long. But come, we must move." And we mended our pace along the lane.

The lane, by the bye, was hard and firm, with scarcely a spot where a track might be left, except in places at the sides; and at these places Hewitt never gave a glance. At the end the lane turned into a by-road, and at the turning Hewitt stopped and scrutinised the ground closely. There was nothing like a recognisable footmark to be seen; but almost immediately Hewitt turned off to the right, and we continued our brisk march without a glance at the road.

"How did you judge which way to turn then?" I asked.

"Didn't you see?" replied Hewitt; "I'll show you at the next turning."

Half a mile farther on the road forked, and here Hewitt stooped and pointed silently to a couple of small twigs, placed crosswise, with the longer twig of the two pointing down the branch of the road to the left. We took the branch to the left, and went on.

"Our man's making a mistake," Hewitt observed. "He leaves his friends' messages lying about for his enemies to read."

We hurried forward with scarcely a word. I was almost too bewildered by what Hewitt had said and done to formulate anything like a reasonable guess as to what our expedition tended, or even to make an effective inquiry—though, after what Hewitt had said, I knew that would be useless. Who was this mysterious man with the broken shoe? what had he to do with the murder of Sneathy? what did the mutilation mean? and who were his friends who left him signs and messages by means of crossed twigs?

We met a man, by whom I sent a short note to my uncle, and soon after we turned into a main road. Here again, at the corner, was the curious message of twigs. A cart-wheel had passed over and crushed them, but it had not so far displaced them as to cause any doubt that the direction to take was to the right. At an inn a little farther along we entered, and Hewitt bought a pint of Irish whisky and a flat bottle to hold it in, as well as a loaf of bread and some cheese, which we carried away wrapped in paper.

"This will have to do for our dinner," Hewitt said as we emerged.

"But we're not going to drink a pint of common whisky between us?" I asked in some astonishment.

"Never mind," Hewitt answered with a smile. "Perhaps we'll find somebody to help us—somebody not so fastidious as yourself as to quality."

Now we hurried—hurried more than ever, for it was beginning to get dusk, and Hewitt feared a difficulty in finding and reading the twig signs in the dark. Two more turnings we made, each with its silent direction—the crossed twigs. To me there was something almost weird and creepy in this curious hunt for the invisible and incomprehensible, guided faithfully and persistently at every turn by this now unmistakable signal. After the second turning we broke into a trot along a long, winding lane, but presently Hewitt's hand fell on my shoulder, and we stopped. He pointed ahead, where some large object, round a bend of the hedge was illuminated as though by a light from below.

"We will walk now," Hewitt said. "Remember that we are on a walking tour, and have come along here entirely by accident."

We proceeded at a swinging walk, Hewitt whistling gaily. Soon we turned the bend, and saw that the large object was a travelling van drawn up with two others on a space of grass by the side of the lane. It was a gipsy encampment, the caravan having apparently only lately stopped, for a man was still engaged in tugging at the rope of a tent that stood near the vans. Two or three sullen-looking ruffians lay about a fire which burned in the space left in the middle of the encampment. A woman stood at the door of one van with a large kettle in her hand, and at the foot of the steps below her a more pleasant-looking old man sat on an inverted pail. Hewitt swung towards the fire from the road, and with an indescribable mixture of slouch, bow, and smile addressed the company generally with "Kooshto bock, pals!"*

[* "Good luck, brothers!"]

The men on the ground took no notice, but continued to stare doggedly before them. The man working at the tent looked round quickly for a moment, and the old man on the bucket looked up and nodded.

Quick to see the most likely friend, Hewitt at once went up to the old man, extending his hand, "Sarshin, daddo!" he said; "Dell mandy tooty's varst."*

[* "How do you do, father? Give me your hand."]

The old man smiled and shook hands, though without speaking. Then Hewitt proceeded, producing the flat bottle of whisky, "Tatty for pawny, chals. Dell mandy the pawny, and lell posh the tatty."*

[* "Spirits for water, lads. Give me the water and take your share of the spirits."]

The whisky did it. We were Romany ryes in twenty minutes or less, and had already been taking tea with the gipsies for half the time. The two or three we had found about the fire were still reserved, but these, I found, were only half-gipsies, and understood very little Romany. One or two others, however, including the old man, were of purer breed, and talked freely, as did one of the women. They were Lees, they said, and expected to be on Wirksby racecourse in three days' time. We, too, were pirimengroes, or travellers, Hewitt explained, and might look to see them on the course.

Then he fell to telling gipsy stories, and they to telling others back, to my intense mystification. Hewitt explained afterwards that they were mostly stories of poaching, with now and again a horse-coping anecdote thrown in. Since then I have learned enough of Romany to take my part in such a conversation, but at the time a word or two here and there was all I could understand. In all this talk the man we had first noticed stretching the tent-rope took very little interest, but lay, with his head away from the fire, smoking his pipe. He was a much darker man than any other present—had, in fact, the appearance of a man of even a swarthier race than that of the others about us.

Presently, in the middle of a long and, of course, to me unintelligible story by the old man, I caught Hewitt's eye. He lifted one eyebrow almost imperceptibly, and glanced for a single moment at his walking-stick. Then I saw that it was pointed toward the feet of the very dark man, who had not yet spoken. One leg was thrown over the others as he lay, with the soles of his shoes presented toward the fire, and in its glare I saw—that the right sole was worn and broken, and that a small triangular tag of leather was doubled over beneath in just the place we knew of from the prints in Ratherby Wood.

I could not take my eyes off that man with his broken shoe. There lay the secret, the whole mystery of the fantastic crime in Ratherby Wood centred in that shabby ruffian. What was it?

But Hewitt went on, talking and joking furiously. The men who were not speaking mostly smoked gloomily, but whenever one spoke, he became animated and lively. I had attempted once or twice to join in, though my efforts were not particularly successful, except in inducing one man to offer me tobacco from his box—tobacco that almost made me giddy in the smell. He tried some of mine in exchange, and though he praised it with native politeness, and smoked the pipe through, I could see that my Hignett mixture was poor stuff in his estimation, compared with the awful tobacco in his own box.

Presently the man with the broken shoe got up, slouched over to his tent, and disappeared. Then said Hewitt (I translate):

"You're not all Lees here, I see?"

"Yes, pal, all Lees."

"But he's not a Lee?" and Hewitt jerked his head towards the tent.

"Why not a Lee, pal? We be Lees, and he is with us. Thus he is a Lee."

"Oh yes, of course. But I know he is from over the pawny. Come, I'll guess the tem* he comes from—it's from Roumania, eh? Perhaps the Wallachian part?"

[* Country]

The men looked at one another, and then the old Lee said:

"You're right, pal. You're cleverer than we took you for. That is what they calls his tem. He is a petulengro*, and he comes with us to shoe the gries** and mend the vardoes***. But he is with us, and so he is a Lee."

[* Smith]
[** Horses]
[*** Vans]

The talk and the smoke went on, and presently the man with the broken shoe returned, and lay down again. Then, when the whisky had all gone, and Hewitt, with some excuse that I did not understand, had begged a piece of cord from one of the men, we left in a chorus of kooshto rardies*.

[* Good-night]

By this time it was nearly ten o'clock. We walked briskly till we came back again to the inn where we had bought the whisky. Here Hewitt, after some little trouble, succeeded in hiring a village cart, and while the driver was harnessing the horse, cut a couple of short sticks from the hedge. These, being each divided into two, made four short, stout pieces of something less than six inches long apiece. Then Hewitt joined them together in pairs, each pair being connected from centre to centre by about nine or ten inches of the cord he had brought from the gipsies' camp. These done, he handed one pair to me. "Handcuffs," he explained, "and no bad ones either. See—you use them so." And he passed the cord round my wrist, gripping the two handles, and giving them a slight twist that sufficiently convinced me of the excruciating pain that might be inflicted by a vigorous turn, and the utter helplessness of a prisoner thus secured in the hands of captors prepared to use their instruments.

"Whom are these for?" I asked. "The man with the broken shoe?"

Hewitt nodded.

"Yes," he said. "I expect we shall find him out alone about midnight. You know how to use these now."

It was fully eleven before the cart was ready and we started. A quarter of a mile or so from the gipsy encampment Hewitt stopped the cart and gave the driver instructions to wait. We got through the hedge, and made our way on the soft ground behind it in the direction of the vans and the tent.

"Roll up your handkerchief," Hewitt whispered, "into a tight pad. The moment I grab him, ram it into his mouth—well in, mind, so that it doesn't easily fall out. Probably he will be stooping—that will make it easier; we can pull him suddenly backward. Now be quiet."

We kept on till nothing but the hedge divided us from the space whereon stood the encampment. It was now nearer twelve o'clock than eleven, but the time we waited seemed endless. But time is not eternity after all, and at last we heard a move in the tent. A minute after, the man we sought was standing before us. He made straight for a gap in the hedge which we had passed on our way, and we crouched low and waited. He emerged on our side of the hedge with his back towards us, and began walking, as we had walked, behind the hedge, but in the opposite direction. We followed.

He carried something in his hand that looked like a large bundle of sticks and twigs, and he appeared to be as anxious to be secret as we ourselves. From time to time he stopped and listened; fortunately there was no moon, or in turning about, as he did once or twice, he would probably have observed us. The field sloped downward just before us, and there was another hedge at right angles, leading down to a slight hollow. To this hollow the man made his way, and in the shade of the new hedge we followed. Presently he stopped suddenly, stooped, and deposited his bundle on the ground before him. Crouching before it, he produced matches from his pocket, struck one, and in a moment had a fire of twigs and small branches, that sent up a heavy white smoke. What all this portended I could not imagine, but a sense of the weirdness of the whole adventure came upon me unchecked. The horrible corpse in the wood, with its severed wrist, Hewitt's enigmatical forebodings, the mysterious tracking of the man with the broken shoe, the scene round the gipsies' fire, and now the strange behaviour of this man, whose connection with the tragedy was so intimate and yet so inexplicable—all these things contributed to make up a tale of but a few hours' duration, but of an inscrutable impressiveness that I began to feel in my nerves.

The man bent a thin stick double, and using it as a pair of tongs, held some indistinguishable object over the flames before him. Excited as I was, I could not help noticing that he bent and held the stick with his left hand. We crept stealthily nearer, and as I stood scarcely three yards behind him and looked over his shoulder, the form of the object stood out clear and black against the dull red of the flame. It was a human hand.

I suppose I may have somehow betrayed my amazement and horror to my companion's sharp eyes, for suddenly I felt his hand tightly grip my arm just above the elbow. I turned, and found his face close by mine and his finger raised warningly. Then I saw him produce his wrist-grip and make a motion with his palm toward his mouth, which I understood to be intended to remind me of the gag. We stepped forward.

The man turned his horrible cookery over and over above the crackling sticks, as though to smoke and dry it in every part. I saw Hewitt's hand reach out toward him, and in a flash we had pulled him back over his heels and I had driven the gag between his teeth as he opened his mouth. We seized his wrists in the cords at once, and I shall never forget the man's look of ghastly, frantic terror as he lay on the ground. When I knew more I understood the reason of this.

Hewitt took both wristholds in one hand and drove the gag entirely into the man's mouth, so that he almost choked. A piece of sacking lay near the fire, and by Hewitt's request I dropped that awful hand from the wooden twigs upon it and rolled it up in a parcel—it was, no doubt, what the sacking had been brought for. Then we lifted the man to his feet and hurried him in the direction of the cart. The whole capture could not have occupied thirty seconds, and as I stumbled over the rough field at the man's left elbow I could only think of the thing as one thinks of a dream that one knows all the time is a dream.

But presently the man, who had been walking quietly, though gasping, sniffing and choking because of the tightly rolled handkerchief in his mouth—presently he made a sudden dive, thinking doubtless to get his wrists free by surprise. But Hewitt was alert, and gave them a twist that made him roll his head with a dismal, stifled yell, and with the opening of his mouth, by some chance the gag fell away. Immediately the man roared aloud for help.

"Quick," said Hewitt, "drag him along—they'll hear in the vans. Bring the hand!"

I seized the fallen handkerchief and crammed it over the man's mouth as well as I might, and together we made as much of a trot as we could, dragging the man between us, while Hewitt checked any reluctance on his part by a timely wrench of the wristholds. It was a hard two hundred and fifty yards to the lane even for us—for the gipsy it must have been a bad minute and a half indeed. Once more as we went over the uneven ground he managed to get out a shout, and we thought we heard a distinct reply from somewhere in the direction of the encampment.

We pulled him over a stile in a tangle, and dragged and pushed him through a small hedge-gap all in a heap. Here we were but a short distance from the cart, and into that we flung him without wasting time or tenderness, to the intense consternation of the driver, who, I believe, very nearly set up a cry for help on his own account. Once in the cart, however, I seized the reins and the whip myself and, leaving Hewitt to take care of the prisoner, put the turn-out along toward Ratherby at as near ten miles an hour as it could go.

We made first for Mr. Hardwick's, but he, we found, was with my uncle, so we followed him. The arrest of the Fosters had been effected, we learned, not very long after we had left the wood, as they returned by another route to Ranworth. We brought our prisoner into the Colonel's library, where he and Mr. Hardwick were sitting.

"I'm not quite sure what we can charge him with unless it's anatomical robbery," Hewitt remarked, "but here's the criminal."

The man only looked down, with a sulkily impenetrable countenance. Hewitt spoke to him once or twice, and at last he said, in a strange accent, something that sounded like "kekin jinnavvy."

"Keck jin?"* asked Hewitt, in the loud, clear tone one instinctively adopts in talking to a foreigner, "Keckeno jinny?"

[* "Not understand?"]

The man understood and shook his head, but not another word would he say or another question answer.

"He's a foreign gipsy," Hewitt explained, "just as I thought—a Wallachian, in fact. Theirs is an older and purer dialect than that of the English gipsies, and only some of the root-words are alike. But I think we can make him explain to-morrow that the Fosters at least had nothing to do with, at any rate, cutting off Sneathy's hand. Here it is, I think." And he gingerly lifted the folds of sacking from the ghastly object as it lay on the table, and then covered it up again.

"But what—what does it all mean?" Mr. Hardwick said in bewildered astonishment. "Do you mean this man was an accomplice?"

"Not at all—the case was one of suicide, as I think you'll agree, when I've explained. This man simply found the body hanging and stole the hand."

"But what in the world for?"

"For the HAND OF GLORY. Eh?" He turned to the gipsy and pointed to the hand on the table: "Yag-varst* eh?"

[Fire-hand.]*

There was a quick gleam of intelligence in the man's eye, but he said nothing. As for myself I was more than astounded. Could it be possible that the old superstition of the Hand of Glory remained alive in a practical shape at this day?

"You know the superstition, of course," Hewitt said. "It did exist in this country in the last century, when there were plenty of dead men hanging at cross-roads, and so on. On the Continent, in some places, it has survived later. Among the Wallachian gipsies it has always been a great article of belief, and the superstition is quite active still. The belief is that the right hand of a hanged man, cut off and dried over the smoke of certain wood and herbs, and then provided with wicks at each finger made of the dead man's hair, becomes, when lighted at each wick (the wicks are greased, of course), a charm, whereby a thief may walk without hinderance where he pleases in a strange house, push open all doors and take what he likes. Nobody can stop him, for everybody the Hand of Glory approaches is made helpless, and can neither move nor speak. You may remember there was some talk of 'thieves' candles' in connection with the horrible series of Whitechapel murders not long ago. That is only one form of the cult of the Hand of Glory."

"Yes," my uncle said; "I remember reading so. There is a story about it in the Ingoldsby Legends, too, I believe."

"There is—it is called 'The Hand of Glory,' in fact. You remember the spell, 'Open lock to the dead man's knock,' and so on. But I think you'd better have the constable up and get this man into safe quarters for the night. He should be searched, of course. I expect they will find on him the hair I noticed to have been cut from Sneathy's head."

The village constable arrived with his iron handcuffs in substitution for those of cord which had so sorely vexed the wrists of our prisoner, and marched him away to the little lock-up on the green.

Then my uncle and Mr. Hardwick turned on Martin Hewitt with doubts and many questions:

"Why do you call it suicide?" Mr. Hardwick asked. "It is plain the Fosters were with him at the time from the tracks. Do you mean to say that they stood there and watched Sneathy hang himself without interfering?"

"No, I don't," Hewitt replied, lighting a cigar. "I think I told you that they never saw Sneathy."

"Yes, you did, and of course that's what they said themselves when they were arrested. But the thing's impossible. Look at the tracks!"

"The tracks are exactly what revealed to me that it was not impossible," Hewitt returned. "I'll tell you how the case unfolded itself to me from the beginning. As to the information you gathered from the Ranworth coachman, to begin with. The conversation between the Fosters which he overheard might well mean something less serious than murder. What did they say? They had been sent for in a hurry and had just had a short consultation with their mother and sister. Henry said that 'the thing must be done at once'; also that as there were two of them it should be easy. Robert said that Henry, as a doctor, would know best what to do.

"Now you, Colonel Brett, had been saying—before we learned these things from Mr. Hardwick—that Sneathy's behaviour of late had become so bad as to seem that of a madman. Then there was the story of his sudden attack on a tradesman in the village, and equally sudden running away—exactly the sort of impulsive, wild thing that madmen do. Why then might it not be reasonable to suppose that Sneathy had become mad—more especially considering all the circumstances of the case, his commercial ruin and disgrace and his horrible life with his wife and her family?—had become suddenly much worse and quite uncontrollable, so that the two wretched women left alone with him were driven to send in haste for Henry and Robert to help them? That would account for all.

"The brothers arrive just after Sneathy had gone out. They are told in a hurried interview how affairs stand, and it is decided that Sneathy must be at once secured and confined in an asylum before something serious happens. He has just gone out—something terrible may be happening at this moment. The brothers determine to follow at once and secure him wherever he may be. Then the meaning of their conversation is plain. The thing that 'must be done, and at once,' is the capture of Sneathy and his confinement in an asylum. Henry, as a doctor, would 'know what to do' in regard to the necessary formalities. And they took a halter in case a struggle should ensue and it were found necessary to bind him. Very likely, wasn't it?"

"Well, yes," Mr. Hardwick replied, "it certainly is. It never struck me in that light at all."

"That was because you believed, to begin with, that a murder had been committed, and looked at the preliminary circumstances which you learned after in the light of your conviction. But now, to come to my actual observations. I saw the footmarks across the fields, and agreed with you (it was indeed obvious) that Sneathy had gone that way first, and that the brothers had followed, walking over his tracks. This state of the tracks continued until well into the wood, when suddenly the tracks of the brothers opened out and proceeded on each side of Sneathy's. The simple inference would seem to be, of course, the one you made—that the Fosters had here overtaken Sneathy, and walked one at each side of him.

"But of this I felt by—no means certain. Another very simple explanation was available, which might chance to be the true one. It was just at the spot where the brothers' tracks separated that the path became suddenly much muddier, because of the closer overhanging of the trees at the spot. The path was, as was to be expected, wettest in the middle. It would be the most natural thing in the world for two well-dressed young men, on arriving here, to separate so as to walk one on each side of the mud in the middle.

"On the other hand, a man in Sneathy's state (assuming him, for the moment, to be mad and contemplating suicide) would walk straight along the centre of the path, taking no note of mud or anything else. I examined all the tracks very carefully, and my theory was confirmed. The feet of the brothers had everywhere alighted in the driest spots, and the steps were of irregular lengths—which meant, of course, that they were picking their way; while Sneathy's footmarks had never turned aside even for the dirtiest puddle. Here, then, were the rudiments of a theory.

"At the watercourse, of course, the footmarks ceased, because of the hard gravel. The body lay on a knoll at the left—a knoll covered with grass. On this the signs of footmarks were almost undiscoverable, although I am often able to discover tracks in grass that are invisible to others. Here, however, it was almost useless to spend much time in examination, for you and your man had been there, and what slight marks there might be would be indistinguishable one from another.

"Under the branch from which the man had hung there was an old tree stump, with a flat top, where the tree had been sawn off. I examined this, and it became fairly apparent that Sneathy had stood on it when the rope was about his neck—his muddy footprint was plain to see; the mud was not smeared about, you see, as it probably would have been if he had been stood there forcibly and pushed off. It was a simple, clear footprint—another hint at suicide.

"But then arose the objection that you mentioned yourself. Plainly the brothers Foster were following Sneathy, and came this way. Therefore, if he hanged himself before they arrived, it would seem that they must have come across the body. But now I examined the body itself. There was mud on the knees, and clinging to one knee was a small leaf. It was a leaf corresponding to those on the bush behind the tree, and it was not a dead leaf, so must have been just detached.

"After my examination of the body I went to the bush, and there, in the thick of it, were, for me, sufficiently distinct knee-marks, in one of which the knee had crushed a spray of the bush against the ground, and from that spray a leaf was missing. Behind the knee-marks were the indentations of boot-toes in the soft, bare earth under the bush, and thus the thing was plain. The poor lunatic had come in sight of the dangling rope, and the temptation to suicide was irresistible. To people in a deranged state of mind the mere sight of the means of self-destruction is often a temptation impossible to withstand. But at that moment he must have heard the steps—probably the voices—of the brothers behind him on the winding path. He immediately hid in the bush till they had passed. It is probable that seeing who the men were, and conjecturing that they were following him—thinking also, perhaps, of things that had occurred between them and himself—his inclination to self-destruction became completely ungovernable, with the result that you saw.

"But before I inspected the bush I noticed one or two more things about the body. You remember I inquired if either of the brothers Foster was left-handed, and was assured that neither was. But clearly the hand had been cut off by a left-handed man, with a large, sharply pointed knife. For well away to the right of where the wrist had hung the knife-point had made a tiny triangular rent in the coat, so that the hand must have been held in the mutilator's right hand, while he used the knife with his left—clearly a left-handed man.

"But most important of all about the body was the jagged hair over the right ear. Everywhere else the hair was well cut and orderly—here it seemed as though a good piece had been, so to speak, sawn off. What could anybody want with a dead man's right hand and certain locks of his hair? Then it struck me suddenly—the man was hanged; it was the Hand of Glory!

"Then you will remember I went, at your request, to see the footprints of the Fosters on the part of the path past the watercourse. Here again it was muddy in the middle, and the two brothers had walked as far apart as before, although nobody had walked between them. A final proof, if one were needed, of my theory as to the three lines of footprints.

"Now I was to consider how to get at the man who had taken his hand. He should be punished for the mutilation, but beyond that he would be required as a witness. Now all the foot-tracks in the vicinity had been accounted for. There were those of the brothers and of Sneathy, which we have been speaking of; those of the rustics looking on, which, however, stopped a little way off, and did not interfere with our sphere of observation; those of your man, who had cut straight through the wood when he first saw the body, and had come back the same way with you; and our own, which we had been careful to keep away from the others. Consequently there was no track of the man who had cut off the hand; therefore it was certain that he must have come along the hard gravel by the watercourse, for that was the only possible path which would not tell the tale. Indeed, it seemed quite a likely path through the wood for a passenger to take, coming from the high ground by the Shopperton road.

"Brett and I left you and traversed the watercourse, both up and down. We found a footprint at the top, left lately by a man with a broken shoe. Right down to the bottom of the watercourse where it emerged from the wood there was no sign on either side of this man having left the gravel. (Where the body was, as you will remember, he would simply have stepped off the gravel on to the grass, which I thought it useless to examine, as I have explained.) But at the bottom, by the lane, the footprint appeared again.

"This then was the direction in which I was to search for a left-handed man with a broken-soled shoe, probably a gipsy—and most probably a foreign gipsy—because a foreign gipsy would be the most likely still to hold the belief in the Hand of Glory. I conjectured the man to be a straggler from a band of gipsies—one who probably had got behind the caravan and had made a short cut across the wood after it; so at the end of the lane I looked for a patrin. This is a sign that gipsies leave to guide stragglers following up. Sometimes it is a heap of dead leaves, sometimes a few stones, sometimes a mark on the ground, but more usually a couple of twigs crossed, with the longer twig pointing the road.

"Guided by these patrins we came in the end on the gipsy camp just as it was settling down for the night. We made ourselves agreeable (as Brett will probably describe to you better than I can), we left them, and after they had got to sleep we came back and watched for the gentleman who is now in the lock-up. He would, of course, seize the first opportunity of treating his ghastly trophy in the prescribed way, and I guessed he would choose midnight, for that is the time the superstition teaches that the hand should be prepared. We made a few small preparations, collared him, and now you've got him. And I should think the sooner you let the brothers Foster go the better."

"But why didn't you tell me all the conclusions you had arrived at at the time?" asked Mr. Hardwick.

"Well, really," Hewitt replied, with a quiet smile, "you were so positive, and some of the traces I relied on were so small, that it would probably have meant a long argument and a loss of time. But more than that, confess, if I had told you bluntly that Sneathy's hand had been taken away to make a mediaeval charm to enable a thief to pass through a locked door and steal plate calmly under the owner's nose, what would you have said?"

"Well, well, perhaps I should have been a little sceptical. Appearances combined so completely to point to the Fosters as murderers that any other explanation almost would have seemed unlikely to me, and that—well no, I confess, I shouldn't have believed in it. But it is a startling thing to find such superstitions alive now-a-days."

"Yes, perhaps it is. Yet we find survivals of the sort very frequently. The Wallachians, however, are horribly superstitious still—the gipsies among them are, of course, worse. Don't you remember the case reported a few months ago, in which a child was drowned as a sacrifice in Wallachia in order to bring rain? And that was not done by gipsies either. Even in England, as late as 1865, a poor paralysed Frenchman was killed by being 'swum' for witchcraft—that was in Essex. And less atrocious cases of belief in wizardry occur again and again even now."

Then Mr. Hardwick and my uncle fell into a discussion as to how the gipsy in the lock-up could be legally punished. Mr. Hardwick thought it should be treated as a theft of a portion of a dead body, but my uncle fancied there was a penalty for mutilation of a dead body per se, though he could not point to the statute. As it happened, however, they were saved the trouble of arriving at a decision, for in the morning he was discovered to have escaped. He had been left, of course, with free hands, and had occupied the night in wrenching out the bars at the top of the back wall of the little prison-shed (it had stood on the green for a hundred and fifty years) and climbing out. He was not found again, and a month or two later the Foster family left the district entirely.

V. — THE CASE OF LAKER, ABSCONDED

There were several of the larger London banks and insurance offices from which Hewitt held a sort of general retainer as detective adviser, in fulfilment of which he was regularly consulted as to the measures to be taken in different cases of fraud, forgery, theft, and so forth, which it might be the misfortune of the particular firms to encounter. The more important and intricate of these cases were placed in his hands entirely, with separate commissions, in the usual way. One of the most important companies of the sort was the General Guarantee Society, an insurance corporation which, among other risks, took those of the integrity of secretaries, clerks, and cashiers. In the case of a cash-box elopement on the part of any person guaranteed by the society, the directors were naturally anxious for a speedy capture of the culprit, and more especially of the booty, before too much of it was spent, in order to lighten the claim upon their funds, and in work of this sort Hewitt was at times engaged, either in general advice and direction or in the actual pursuit of the plunder and the plunderer.

Arriving at his office a little later than usual one morning, Hewitt found an urgent message awaiting him from the General Guarantee Society, requesting his attention to a robbery which had taken place on the previous day. He had gleaned some hint of the case from the morning paper, wherein appeared a short paragraph, which ran thus:

SERIOUS BANK ROBBERY.—In the course of yesterday a clerk employed by Messrs Liddle, Neal & Liddle, the well-known bankers, disappeared, having in his possession a large sum of money, the property of his employers—a sum reported to be rather over £15,000. It would seem that he had been entrusted to collect the money in his capacity of 'walk-clerk' from various other banks and trading concerns during the morning, but failed to return at the usual time. A large number of the notes which he received had been cashed at the Bank of England before suspicion was aroused. We understand that Detective-Inspector Plummer, of Scotland Yard, has the case in hand.

The clerk, whose name was Charles William Laker, had, it appeared from the message, been guaranteed in the usual way by the General Guarantee Society, and Hewitt's presence at the office was at once desired in order that steps might quickly be taken for the man's apprehension and in the recovery, at any rate, of as much of the booty as possible.

A smart hansom brought Hewitt to Threadneedle Street in a bare quarter of an hour, and there a few minutes' talk with the manager, Mr Lyster, put him in possession of the main facts of the case, which appeared to be simple. Charles William Laker was twenty-five years of age, and had been in the employ of Messrs Liddle, Neal & Liddle for something more than seven years—since he left school, in fact—and until the previous day there had been nothing in his conduct to complain of. His duties as walk-clerk consisted in making a certain round, beginning at about half-past ten each morning. There were a certain number of the more important banks between which and Messrs Liddle, Neal & Liddle there were daily transactions, and a few smaller semi-private banks and merchant firms acting as financial agents with whom there was business intercourse of less importance and regularity; and each of these, as necessary, he visited in turn, collecting cash due on bills and other instruments of a like nature. He carried a wallet, fastened securely to his person by a chain, and this wallet contained the bills and the cash. Usually at the end of his round, when all his bills had been converted into cash, the wallet held very large sums. His work and responsibilities, in fine, were those common to walk-clerks in all banks.

On the day of the robbery he had started out as usual—possibly a little earlier than was customary—and the bills and other securities in his possession represented considerably more than £15,000.

It had been ascertained that he had called in the usual way at each establishment on the round, and had transacted his business at the last place by about a quarter-past one, being then, without doubt, in possession of cash to the full value of the bills negotiated. After that, Mr Lyster said, yesterday's report was that nothing more had been heard of him. But this morning there had been a message to the effect that he had been traced out of the country—to Calais, at least, it was thought. The directors of the society wished Hewitt to take the case in hand personally and at once, with a view of recovering what was possible from the plunder by way of salvage; also, of course, of finding Laker, for it is an important moral gain to guarantee societies, as an example, if a thief is caught and punished. Therefore Hewitt and Mr Lyster, as soon as might be, made for Messrs Liddle, Neal & Liddle's, that the investigation might be begun.

The bank premises were quite near—in Leadenhall Street. Having arrived there, Hewitt and Mr Lyster made their way to the firm's private rooms. As they were passing an outer waiting-room, Hewitt noticed two women. One, the elder, in widow's weeds, was sitting with her head bowed in her hand over a small writing-table. Her face was not visible, but her whole attitude was that of a person overcome with unbearable grief; and she sobbed quietly. The other was a young woman of twenty-two or twenty-three. Her thick black veil revealed no more than that her features were small and regular and that her face was pale and drawn. She stood with a hand on the elder woman's shoulder, and she quickly turned her head away as the two men entered.

Mr Neal, one of the partners, received them in his own room. 'Good-morning, Mr Hewitt,' he said, when Mr Lyster had introduced the detective. 'This is a serious business—very. I think I am sorrier for Laker himself than for anybody else, ourselves included—or, at any rate, I am sorrier for his mother. She is waiting now to see Mr Liddle, as soon as he arrives—Mr Liddle has known the family for a long time. Miss Shaw is with her, too, poor girl. She is a governess, or something of that sort, and I believe she and Laker were engaged to be married. It's all very sad.'

'Inspector Plummer, I understand,' Hewitt remarked, 'has the affair in hand, on behalf of the police?'

'Yes,' Mr Neal replied; 'in fact, he's here now, going through the contents of Laker's desk, and so forth; he thinks it possible Laker may have had accomplices. Will you see him?'

'Presently. Inspector Plummer and I are old friends. We met last, I think, in the case of the Stanway cameo, some months ago. But, first, will you tell me how long Laker has been a walk-clerk?'

'Barely four months, although he has been with us altogether seven years. He was promoted to the walk soon after the beginning of the year.'

'Do you know anything of his habits—what he used to do in his spare time, and so forth?'

'Not a great deal. He went in for boating, I believe, though I have heard it whispered that he had one or two more expensive tastes—expensive, that is, for a young man in his position,' Mr Neal explained, with a dignified wave of the hand that he peculiarly affected. He was a stout old gentleman, and the gesture suited him.

'You have had no reason to suspect him of dishonesty before, I take it?'

'Oh, no. He made a wrong return once, I believe, that went for some time undetected, but it turned out, after all, to be a clerical error—a mere clerical error.'

'Do you know anything of his associates out of the office?'

'No, how should I? I believe Inspector Plummer has been making inquiries as to that, however, of the other clerks. Here he is, by the bye, I expect. Come in!'

It was Plummer who had knocked, and he came in at Mr Neal's call. He was a middle-sized, small-eyed, impenetrable-looking man, as yet of no great reputation in the force. Some of my readers may remember his connection with that case, so long a public mystery, that I have elsewhere fully set forth and explained under the title of 'The Stanway Cameo Mystery'. Plummer carried his billy-cock hat in one hand and a few papers in the other. He gave Hewitt good-morning, placed his hat on a chair, and spread the papers on the table.

'There's not a great deal here,' he said, 'but one thing's plain—Laker had been betting. See here, and here, and here'—he took a few letters from the bundle in his hand—'two letters from a bookmaker about settling—wonder he trusted a clerk—several telegrams from tipsters, and a letter from some friend—only signed by initials—asking Laker to put a sovereign on a horse for the friend "with his own." I'll keep these, I think. It may be worth while to see that friend, if we can find him. Ah, we often find it's betting, don't we, Mr Hewitt? Meanwhile, there's no news from France yet.'

'You are sure that is where he is gone?' asked Hewitt.

'Well, I'll tell you what we've done as yet. First, of course, I went round to all the banks. There was nothing to be got from that. The cashiers all knew him by sight, and one was a personal friend of his. He had called as usual, said nothing in particular, cashed his bills in the ordinary way, and finished up at the Eastern Consolidated Bank at about a quarter-past one. So far there was nothing whatever. But I had started two or three men meanwhile making inquiries at the railway stations, and so on. I had scarcely left the Eastern Consolidated when one of them came after me with news. He had tried Palmer's Tourist Office, although that seemed an unlikely place, and there struck the track.'

'Had he been there?'

'Not only had he been there, but he had taken a tourist ticket for France. It was quite a smart move, in a way. You see it was the sort of ticket that lets you do pretty well what you like; you have the choice of two or three different routes to begin with, and you can break your journey where you please, and make all sorts of variations. So that a man with a ticket like that, and a few hours' start, could twist about on some remote branch route, and strike off in another direction altogether, with a new ticket, from some out-of-the-way place, while we were carefully sorting out and inquiring along the different routes he might have taken. Not half a bad move for a new hand; but he made one bad mistake, as new hands always do—as old hands do, in fact, very often. He was fool enough to give his own name, C. Laker! Although that didn't matter much, as the description was enough to fix him.

There he was, wallet and all, just as he had come from the Eastern Consolidated Bank. He went straight from there to Palmer's, by the bye, and probably in a cab. We judge that by the time. He left the Eastern Consolidated at a quarter-past one, and was at Palmer's by twenty-five-past—ten minutes. The clerk at Palmer's remembered the time because he was anxious to get out to his lunch, and kept looking at the clock, expecting another clerk in to relieve him. Laker didn't take much in the way of luggage, I fancy. We inquired carefully at the stations, and got the porters to remember the passengers for whom they had been carrying luggage, but none appeared to have had any dealings with our man. That, of course, is as one would expect. He'd take as little as possible with him, and buy what he wanted on the way, or when he'd reached his hiding-place. Of course, I wired to Calais (it was a Dover to Calais route ticket) and sent a couple of smart men off by the 8.15 mail from Charing Cross. I expect we shall hear from them in the course of the day. I am being kept in London in view of something expected at headquarters, or I should have been off myself.'

'That is all, then, up to the present? Have you anything else in view?'

'That', all I've absolutely ascertained at present. As for what I'm going to do'—a slight smile curled Plummer's lip—' well, I shall see. I've a thing or two in my mind.'

Hewitt smiled slightly himself; he recognized Plummer's touch of professional jealousy. 'Very well,' he said, rising, 'I'll make an inquiry or two for myself at once. Perhaps, Mr Neal, you'll allow one of your clerks to show me the banks, in their regular order, at which Laker called yesterday. I think I'll begin at the beginning.'

Mr Neal offered to place at Hewitt's disposal anything or anybody the bank contained, and the conference broke up. As Hewitt, with the clerk, came through the rooms separating Mr Neal's sanctum from the outer office, lie fancied he saw the two veiled women leaving by a side door.

The first bank was quite close to Liddle, Neal & Liddle's. There the cashier who had dealt with Laker the day before remembered nothing in particular about the interview. Many other walk-clerks had called during the morning, as they did every morning, and the only circumstances of the visit that he could say anything definite about were those recorded in figures in the books. He did not know Laker's name till Plummer had mentioned it in making inquiries on the previous afternoon. As far as he could remember, Laker behaved much as usual, though really he did not notice much; he looked chiefly at the bills. He described Laker in a way that corresponded with the photograph that Hewitt had borrowed from the bank; a young man with a brown moustache and ordinary-looking fairly regular face, dressing much as other clerks dressed—tall hat, black cutaway coat, and so on. The numbers of the notes handed over had already been given to Inspector Plummer, and these Hewitt did not trouble about.

The next bank was in Cornhill, and here the cashier was a personal friend of Laker's—at any rate, an acquaintance—and he remembered a little more. Laker's manner had been quite as usual, he said; certainly he did not seem preoccupied or excited in his manner. He spoke for a moment or two—of being on the river on Sunday, and so on—and left in his usual way.

'Can you remember everything he said?' Hewitt asked. 'If you can tell me, I should like to know exactly what he did and said to the smallest particular.'

'Well, he saw me a little distance off—I was behind there, at one of the desks—and raised his hand to me, and said, "How d'ye do?" I came across and took his bills, and dealt with them in the usual way. He had a new umbrella lying on the counter—rather a handsome umbrella—and I made a remark about the handle. He took it up to show me, and told me it was a present he had just received from a friend. It was a gorse-root handle, with two silver bands, one with his monogram, C.W.L. I said it was a very nice handle, and asked him whether it was fine in his district on Sunday. He said he had been up the river, and it was very fine there. And I think that was all.'

'Thank you. Now about this umbrella. Did he carry it rolled? Can you describe it in detail?'

'Well, I've told you about the handle, and the rest was much as usual, I think; it wasn't rolled—just napping loosely, you know. It was rather an odd-shaped handle, though. I'll try and sketch it, if you like, as well as I can remember.' He did so, and Hewitt saw in the result rough indications of a gnarled crook, with one silver band near the end, and another, with the monogram, a few inches down the handle. Hewitt put the sketch in his pocket, and bade the cashier good-day.

At the next bank the story was the same as at the first—there was nothing remembered but the usual routine. Hewitt and the clerk turned down a narrow paved court, and through into Lombard Street for the next visit. The bank—that of Buller, Clayton, Ladds & Co.—was just at the corner at the end of the court, and the imposing stone entrance-porch was being made larger and more imposing still, the way being almost blocked by ladders and scaffold-poles. Here there was only the usual tale, and so on through the whole walk. The cashiers knew Laker only by sight, and that not always very distinctly. The calls of walk-clerks were such matters of routine that little note was taken of the persons of the clerks themselves, who were called by the names of their firms, if they were called by any names at all. Laker had behaved much as usual, so far as the cashiers could remember, and when finally the Eastern Consolidated was left behind, nothing more had been learnt than the chat about Laker's new umbrella.

Hewitt had taken leave of Mr Neal's clerk, and was stepping into a hansom, when he noticed a veiled woman in widow's weeds hailing another hansom a little way behind. He recognized the figure again, and said to the driver: 'Drive fast to Palmer's Tourist Office, but keep your eye on that cab behind, and tell me presently if it is following us.'

The cabman drove off, and after passing one or two turnings, opened the lid above Hewitt's head, and said: 'That there other keb is a-follerin' us, sir, an' keepin' about even distance all along.'

'All right; that's what I wanted to know. Palmer's now.' At Palmer's the clerk who had attended to Laker remembered him very well and described him. He also remembered the wallet, and thought he remembered the umbrella—was practically sure of it, in fact, upon reflection. He had no record of the name given, but remembered it distinctly to be Laker. As a matter of fact, names were never asked in such a transaction, but in this case Laker appeared to be ignorant of the usual procedure, as well as in a great hurry, and asked for the ticket and gave his name all in one breath, probably assuming that the name would be required.

Hewitt got back to his cab, and started for Charing Cross. The cabman once more lifted the lid and informed him that the hansom with the veiled woman in it was again following, having waited while Hewitt had visited Palmer's. At Charing Cross Hewitt discharged his cab and walked straight to the lost property office. The man in charge knew him very well, for his business had carried him there frequently before.

'I fancy an umbrella was lost in the station yesterday,' Hewitt said. 'It was a new umbrella, silk, with a gnarled gorse-root handle and two silver bands, something like this sketch. There was a monogram on the lower band—"C. W. L." were the letters. Has it been brought here?'

'There was two or three yesterday,' the man said; 'let's see.' He took the sketch and retired to a corner of his room. 'Oh, yes—here it is, I think; isn't this it? Do you claim it?' 'Well, not exactly that, but I think I'll take a look at it, if you'll let me. By the way, I see it's rolled up. Was it found like that?'

'No; the chap rolled it up what found it—porter he was. It's a fad of his, rolling up umbrellas close and neat, and he's rather proud of it. He often looks as though he'd like to take a man's umbrella away and roll it up for him when it's a bit clumsy done. Rum fad, eh?'

'Yes; everybody has his little fad, though. Where was this found—close by here?'

'Yes, sir; just there, almost opposite this window, in the little corner.'

'About two o'clock?'

'Ah, about that time, more or less.'

Hewitt took the umbrella up, unfastened the band, and shook the silk out loose. Then he opened it, and as he did so a small scrap of paper fell from inside it. Hewitt pounced on it like lightning. Then, after examining the umbrella thoroughly, inside and out, he handed it back to the man, who had not observed the incident of the scrap of paper.

'That will do, thanks,' he said. 'I only wanted to take a peep at it—just a small matter connected with a little case of mine. Good-morning.'

He turned suddenly and saw, gazing at him with a terrified expression from a door behind, the face of the woman who had followed him in the cab. The veil was lifted, and he caught but a mere glance of the face ere it was suddenly withdrawn. He stood for a moment to allow the woman time to retreat, and then left the station and walked toward his office, close by.

Scarcely thirty yards along the Strand he met Plummer. 'I'm going to make some much closer inquiries all down the line as far as Dover,' Plummer said. 'They wire from Calais that they have no clue as yet, and I mean to make quite sure, if I can, that Laker hasn't quietly slipped off the line somewhere between here and Dover. There's one very peculiar thing,' Plummer added confidentially. 'Did you see the two women who were waiting to see a member of the firm at Liddle, Neal & Liddle's?'

'Yes. Laker's mother and his fiancée, I was told.'

'That's right. Well, do you know that girl—Shaw her name is—has been shadowing me ever since I left the Bank. Of course I spotted it from the beginning—these amateurs don't know how to follow anybody—and, as a matter of fact, she's just inside that jeweller's shop door behind me now, pretending to look at the things in the window. But it's odd, isn't it?'

'Well,' Hewitt replied, 'of course it's not a thing to be neglected. If you'll look very carefully at the corner of Villiers Street, without appearing to stare, I think you will possibly observe some signs of Laker's mother. She's shadowing me.'

Plummer looked casually in the direction indicated, and then immediately turned his eyes in another direction.

'I see her,' he said; 'she's just taking a look round the corner. That's a thing not to be be ignored. Of course, the Lakers' house is being watched—we set a man on it at once, yesterday. But I'll put some one on now to watch Miss Shaw's place too. I'll telephone through to Liddle's—probably they'll be able to say where it is. And the women themselves must be watched, too. As a matter of fact, I had a notion that Laker wasn't alone in it. And it's just possible, you know, that he has sent an accomplice off with his tourist ticket to lead us a dance while he looks after himself in another direction. Have you done anything?'

'Well,' Hewitt replied, with a faint reproduction of the secretive smile with which Plummer had met an inquiry of his earlier in the morning, 'I've been to the station here, and I've found Laker's umbrella in the lost property office.'

'Oh! Then probably he has gone. I'll bear that in mind, and perhaps have a word with the lost property man.'

Plummer made for the station and Hewitt for his office. He mounted the stairs and reached his door just as I myself, who had been disappointed in not finding him in, was leaving. I had called with the idea of taking Hewitt to lunch with me at my club, but he declined lunch. 'I have an important case in hand,' he said. 'Look here, Brett. See this scrap of paper. You know the types of the different newspapers—which is this?'

He handed me a small piece of paper. It was part of a cutting containing an advertisement, which had been torn in half.

'I think,' I said, 'this is from the Daily Chronicle, judging by the paper. It is plainly from the "agony column", but all the papers use pretty much the same type for these advertisements, except the Times. If it were not torn I could tell you at once, because the Chronicle columns are rather narrow.'

'Never mind—I'll send for them all.' He rang, and sent Kerrett for a copy of each morning paper of the previous day. Then he took from a large wardrobe cupboard a decent but well-worn and rather roughened tall hat. Also a coat a little worn and shiny on the collar. He exchanged these for his own hat and coat, and then substituted an old necktie for his own clean white one, and encased his legs in mud-spotted leggings. This done, he produced a very large and thick pocket-book, fastened by a broad elastic band, and said, 'Well, what do you think of this? Will it do for Queen's taxes, or sanitary inspection, or the gas, or the water-supply?'

'Very well indeed, I should say,' I replied. 'What's the case?'

'Oh, I'll tell you all about that when it's over—no time now. Oh, here you are, Kerrett. By the bye, Kerrett, I'm going out presently by the back way. Wait for about ten minutes or a quarter of an hour after I am gone, and then just go across the road and speak to that lady in black, with the veil, who is waiting in that little foot-passage opposite. Say Mr Martin Hewitt sends his compliments, and he advises her not to wait, as he has already left his office by another door, and has been gone some little time. That's all; it would be a pity to keep the poor woman waiting all day for nothing. Now the papers. Daily News, Standard, Telegraph, Chronicle—yes, here it is, in the Chronicle.'

The whole advertisement read thus:

YOB.—H.R. Shop roast. You 1st. Then
to-night. O2. 2nd top 3rd L. No.197
red bl. straight mon. One at a time.

'What's this,' I asked, 'a cryptogram?'

'I'll see,' Hewitt answered. 'But I won't tell you anything about it till afterwards, so you get your lunch. Kerrett, bring the directory.'

This was all I actually saw of this case myself, and I have written the rest in its proper order from Hewitt's information, as I have written some other cases entirely.

To resume at the point where, for the time, I lost sight of the matter. Hewitt left by the back way and stopped an empty cab as it passed. 'Abney Park Cemetery' was his direction to the driver. In little more than twenty minutes the cab was branching off down the Essex Road on its way to Stoke Newington, and in twenty minutes more Hewitt stopped it in Church Street, Stoke Newington. He walked through a street or two, and then down another, the houses of which he scanned carefully as he passed. Opposite one which stood by itself he stopped, and, making a pretence of consulting and arranging his large pocket-book, he took a good look at the house. It was rather larger, neater, and more pretentious than the others in the street, and it had a natty little coach-house just visible up the side entrance. There were red blinds hung with heavy lace in the front windows, and behind one of these blinds Hewitt was able to catch the glint of a heavy gas chandelier.

He stepped briskly up the front steps and knocked sharply at the door. 'Mr Merston?' he asked, pocket-book in hand, when a neat parlourmaid opened the door.

'Yes.'

'Ah!' Hewitt stepped into the hall and pulled off his hat; 'it's only the meter. There's been a deal of gas running away somewhere here, and I'm just looking to see if the meters are right. Where is it?'

The girl hesitated. 'I'll—I'll ask master,' she said.

'Very well. I don't want to take it away, you know—only to give it a tap or two, and so on.'

The girl retired to the back of the hall, and without taking her eyes off Martin Hewitt, gave his message to some invisible person in a back room, whence came a growling reply of 'All right'.

Hewitt followed the girl to the basement, apparently looking straight before him, but in reality taking in every detail of the place. The gas meter was in a very large lumber cupboard under the kitchen stairs. The girl opened the door and lit a candle. The meter stood on the floor, which was littered with hampers and boxes and odd sheets of brown paper. But a thing that at once arrested Hewitt's attention was a garment of some sort of bright blue cloth, with large brass buttons, which was lying in a tumbled heap in a corner, and appeared to be the only thing in the place that was not covered with dust. Nevertheless, Hewitt took no apparent notice of it, but stooped down and solemnly tapped the meter three times with his pencil, and listened with great gravity, placing his ear to the top. Then he shook his head and tapped again. At length he said:

'It's a bit doubtful. I'll just get you to light the gas in the kitchen a moment. Keep your hand to the burner, and when I call out shut it off at once; see?'

The girl turned and entered the kitchen, and Hewitt immediately seized the blue coat—for a coat it was. It had a dull red piping in the seams, and was of the swallowtail pattern—livery coat, in fact. He held it for a moment before him, examining its pattern and colour, and then rolled it up and flung it again into the corner.

'Right!' he called to the servant. 'Shut off!'

The girl emerged from the kitchen as he left the cupboard.

'Well,' she asked, 'are you satisfied now?'

'Quite satisfied, thank you,' Hewitt replied.

'Is it all right?' she continued, jerking her hand toward the cupboard.

'Well, no, it isn't; there's something wrong there, and I'm glad I came. You can tell Mr Merston, if you like, that I expect his gas bill will be a good deal less next quarter.' And there was a suspicion of a chuckle in Hewitt's voice as he crossed the hall to leave. For a gas inspector is pleased when he finds at length what he has been searching for.

Things had fallen out better than Hewitt had dared to expect. He saw the key of the whole mystery in that blue coat; for it was the uniform coat of the hall porters at one of the banks that he had visited in the morning, though which one he could not for the moment remember. He entered the nearest post-office and despatched a telegram to Plummer, giving certain directions and asking the inspector to meet him; then he hailed the first available cab and hurried toward the City.

At Lombard Street he alighted, and looked in at the door of each bank till he came to Buller, Clayton, Ladds & Co.'s. This was the bank he wanted. In the other banks the hall porters wore mulberry coats, brick-dust coats, brown coats, and what not, but here, behind the ladders and scaffold poles which obscured the entrance, he could see a man in a blue coat, with dull red piping and brass buttons. He sprang up the steps, pushed open the inner swing door, and finally satisfied himself by a closer view of the coat, to the wearer's astonishment. Then he regained the pavement and walked the whole length of the bank premises in front, afterwards turning up the paved passage at the side, deep in thought. The bank had no windows or doors on the side next the court, and the two adjoining houses were old and supported in place by wooden shores. Both were empty, and a great board announced that tenders would be received in a month's time for the purchase of the old materials of which they were constructed; also that some part of the site would be let on a long building lease.

Hewitt looked up at the grimy fronts of the old buildings. The windows were crusted thick with dirt—all except the bottom window of the house nearer the bank, which was fairly clean, and seemed to have been quite lately washed. The door, too, of this house was cleaner than that of the other, though the paint was worn. Hewitt reached and fingered a hook driven into the left-hand doorpost about six feet from the ground. It was new, and not at all rusted; also a tiny splinter had been displaced when the hook was driven in, and clean wood showed at the spot.

Having observed these things, Hewitt stepped back and read at the bottom of the big board the name, 'Winsor & Weekes, Surveyors and Auctioneers, Abchurch Lane'. Then he stepped into Lombard Street.

Two hansoms pulled up near the post-office, and out of the first stepped Inspector Plummer and another man. This man and the two who alighted from the second hansom were unmistakably plain-clothes constables—their air, gait, and boots proclaimed it.

'What's all this?' demanded Plummer, as Hewitt approached.

'You'll soon see, I think. But, first, have you put the watch on No. 197, Hackworth Road?'

'Yes; nobody will get away from there alone.'

'Very good. I am going into Abchurch Lane for a few minutes. Leave your men out here, but just go round into the court by Buller, Clayton & Ladds's, and keep your eye on the first door on the left. I think we'll find something soon. Did you get rid of Miss Shaw?'

'No, she's behind now, and Mrs Laker's with her. They met in the Strand, and came after us in another cab. Rare fun, eh! They think we're pretty green! It's quite handy, too. So long as they keep behind me it saves all trouble of watching them.' And Inspector Plummer chuckled and winked.

'Very good. You don't mind keeping your eye on that door, do you? I'll be back very soon,' and with that Hewitt turned off into Abchurch Lane.

At Winsor & Weekes's information was not difficult to obtain. The houses were destined to come down very shortly, but a week or so ago an office and a cellar in one of them was let temporarily to a Mr Westley. He brought no references; indeed, as he paid a fortnight's rent in advance, he was not asked for any, considering the circumstances of the case. He was opening a London branch for a large firm of cider merchants, he said, and just wanted a rough office and a cool cellar to store samples in for a few weeks till the permanent premises were ready. There was another key, and no doubt the premises might be entered if there were any special need for such a course. Martin Hewitt gave such excellent reasons that Winsor & Weekes's managing clerk immediately produced the key and accompanied Hewitt to the spot.

'I think you'd better have your men handy,' Hewitt remarked to Plummer when they reached the door, and a whistle quickly brought the men over.

The key was inserted in the lock and turned, but the door would not open; the bolt was fastened at the bottom. Hewitt stooped and looked under the door.

'It's a drop bolt,' he said. 'Probably the man who left last let it fall loose, and then banged the door, so that it fell into its place. I must try my best with a wire or a piece of string.'

A wire was brought, and with some manoeuvring Hewitt contrived to pass it round the bolt, and lift it little by little, steadying it with the blade of a pocket-knife. When at length the bolt was raised out of the hole, the knife-blade was slipped under it, and the door swung open.

They entered. The door of the little office just inside stood open, but in the office there was nothing, except a board a couple of feet long in a corner. Hewitt stepped across and lifted this, turning it downward face toward Plummer. On it, in fresh white paint on a black ground, were painted the words—

"Buller, Clayton, Ladds & Co.,
Temporary Entrance."

Hewitt turned to Winsor & Weekes's clerk and asked, 'The man who took this room called himself Westley, didn't he?'

'Yes.'

'Youngish man, clean-shaven, and well-dressed?'

'Yes, he was.'

'I fancy,' Hewitt said, turning to Plummer, 'I fancy an old friend of yours is in this—Mr Sam Gunter.'

'What, the "Hoxton Yob"?'

'I think it's possible he's been Mr Westley for a bit, and somebody else for another bit. But let's come to the cellar.'

Winsor & Weekes's clerk led the way down a steep flight of steps into a dark underground corridor, wherein they lighted their way with many successive matches. Soon the cellar corridor made a turn to the right, and as the party passed the turn, there came from the end of the passage before them a fearful yell.

'Help! help! Open the door! I'm going mad—mad! O my God!'

And there was a sound of desperate beating from the inside of the cellar door at the extreme end. The men stopped, startled.

'Come,' said Hewitt, 'more matches!' and he rushed to the door. It was fastened with a bar and padlock.

'Let me out, for God's sake!' came the voice, sick and hoarse, from the inside. 'Let me out!'

'All right!' Hewitt shouted. 'We have come for you. Wait a moment.'

The voice sank into a sort of sobbing croon, and Hewitt tried several keys from his own bunch on the padlock. None fitted. He drew from his pocket the wire he had used for the bolt of the front door, straightened it out, and made a sharp bend at the end.

'Hold a match close,' he ordered shortly, and one of the men obeyed. Three or four attempts were necessary, and several different bendings of the wire were effected, but in the end Hewitt picked the lock, and flung open the door.

From within a ghastly figure fell forward among them fainting, and knocked out the matches.

'Hullo!' cried Plummer. 'Hold up! Who are you?'

'Let's get him up into the open,' said Hewitt. 'He can't tell you who he is for a bit, but I believe he's Laker.'

'Laker! What, here?'

'I think so. Steady up the steps. Don't bump him. He's pretty sore already, I expect.'

Truly the man was a pitiable sight. His hair and face were caked in dust and blood, and his finger-nails were torn and bleeding. Water was sent for at once, and brandy.

'Well,' said Plummer hazily, looking first at the unconscious prisoner and then at Hewitt, 'but what about the swag?'

'You'll have to find that yourself,' Hewitt replied. 'I think my share of the case is about finished. I only act for the Guarantee Society, you know, and if Laker's proved innocent—'

'Innocent! How?'

'Well, this is what took place, as near as I can figure it. You'd better undo his collar, I think'—this to the men. 'What I believe has happened is this. There has been a very clever and carefully prepared conspiracy here, and Laker has not been the criminal, but the victim.'

'Been robbed himself, you mean? But how? Where?'

'Yesterday morning, before he had been to more than three banks—here, in fact.'

'But then how? You're all wrong. We know he made the whole round, and did all the collection. And then Palmer's office, and all, and the umbrella; why—'

The man lay still unconscious. 'Don't raise his head,' Hewitt said. 'And one of you had best fetch a doctor. He's had a terrible shock.' Then turning to Plummer he went on, 'As to how they managed the job, I'll tell you what I think. First it struck some very clever person that a deal of money might be got by robbing a walk-clerk from a bank. This clever person was one of a clever gang of thieves—perhaps the Hoxton Row gang, as I think I hinted. Now you know quite as well as I do that such a gang will spend any amount of time over a job that promises a big haul, and that for such a job they can always command the necessary capital. There are many most respectable persons living in good style in the suburbs whose chief business lies in financing such ventures, and taking the chief share of the proceeds. Well, this is their plan, carefully and intelligently carried out. They watch Laker, observe the round he takes, and his habits. They find that there is only one of the clerks with whom he does business that he is much acquainted with, and that this clerk is in a bank which is commonly second in Laker's round. The sharpest man among them—and I don't think there's a man in London could do this as well as young Sam Gunter—studies Laker's dress and habits just as an actor studies a character. They take this office and cellar, as we have seen, because it is next door to a bank whose front entrance is being altered—a fact which Laker must know from his daily visits. The smart man—Gunter, let us say, and I have other reasons for believing it to be he—makes up precisely like Laker, false moustache, dress, and everything, and waits here with the rest of the gang. One of the gang is dressed in a blue coat with brass buttons, like a hall-porter in Buller's bank. Do you see?'

'Yes, I think so. It's pretty clear now.'

'A confederate watches at the top of the court, and the moment Laker turns in from Cornhill—having already been, mind, at the only bank where he was so well known that the disguised thief would not have passed muster—as soon as he turns in from Cornhill, I say, a signal is given, and that board'—pointing to that with the white letters—'is hung on the hook in the doorpost. The sham porter stands beside it, and as Laker approaches says, "This way in, sir, this morning. The front way's shut for the alterations." Laker suspecting nothing, and supposing that the firm have made a temporary entrance through the empty house, enters. He is seized when well along the corridor, the board is taken down and the door shut. Probably he is stunned by a blow on the head—see the blood now. They take his wallet and all the cash he has already collected. Gunter takes the wallet and also the umbrella, since it has Laker's initials, and is therefore distinctive. He simply completes the walk in the character of Laker, beginning with Buller, Clayton & Ladds's just round the corner. It is nothing but routine work, which is quickly done, and nobody notices him particularly—it is the bills they examine. Meanwhile this unfortunate fellow is locked up in the cellar here, right at the end of the underground corridor, where he can never make himself heard in the street, and where next him are only the empty cellars of the deserted house next door. The thieves shut the front door and vanish. The rest is plain. Gunter, having completed the round, and bagged some £15,000 or more, spends a few pounds in a tourist ticket at Palmer's as a blind, being careful to give Laker's name. He leaves the umbrella at Charing Cross in a conspicuous place right opposite the lost property office, where it is sure to be seen, and so completes his false trail.'

'Then who are the people at 197, Hackworth Road?'

'The capitalist lives there—the financier, and probably the directing spirit of the whole thing. Merston's the name he goes by there, and I've no doubt he cuts a very imposing figure in chapel every Sunday. He'll be worth picking up—this isn't the first thing he's been in, I'll warrant.'

'But—but what about Laker's mother and Miss Shaw?'

'Well, what? The poor women are nearly out of their minds with terror and shame, that's all, but though they may think Laker a criminal, they'll never desert him. They've been following us about with a feeble, vague sort of hope of being able to baffle us in some way or help him if we caught him, or something, poor things. Did you ever hear of a real woman who'd desert a son or a lover merely because he was a criminal? But here's the doctor. When he's attended to him will you let your men take Laker home? I must hurry and report to the Guarantee Society, I think.'

'But,' said the perplexed Plummer, 'where did you get your clue? You must have had a tip from some one, you know—you can't have done it by clairvoyance. What gave you the tip?'

'The Daily Chronicle.'

'The what?'

'The Daily Chronicle. Just take a look at the "agony column" in yesterday morning's issue, and read the message to "Yob"—to Gunter, in fact. That's all.'

By this time a cab was waiting in Lombard Street, and two of Plummer's men, under the doctor's directions, carried Laker to it. No sooner, however, were they in the court than the two watching women threw themselves hysterically upon Laker, and it was long before they could be persuaded that he was not being taken to gaol. The mother shrieked aloud, 'My boy—my boy! Don't take him! Oh, don't take him! They've killed my boy! Look at his head—oh, his head!' and wrestled desperately with the men, while Hewitt attempted to soothe her, and promised to allow her to go in the cab with her son if she would only be quiet. The younger woman made no noise, but she held one of Laker's limp hands in both hers.

Hewitt and I dined together that evening, and he gave me a full account of the occurrences which I have here set down. Still, when he was finished I was not able to see clearly by what process of reasoning he had arrived at the conclusions that gave him the key to the mystery, nor did I understand the 'agony column' message, and I said so.

'In the beginning,' Hewitt explained, 'the thing that struck me as curious was the fact that Laker was said to have given his own name at Palmer's in buying his ticket. Now, the first thing the greenest and newest criminal thinks of is changing his name, so that the giving of his own name seemed unlikely to begin with. Still, he might have made such a mistake, as Plummer suggested when he said that criminals usually make a mistake somewhere—as they do, in fact. Still, it was the least likely mistake I could think of—especially as he actually didn't wait to be asked for his name, but blurted it out when it wasn't really wanted. And it was conjoined with another rather curious mistake, or what would have been a mistake, if the thief were Laker. Why should he conspicuously display his wallet—such a distinctive article—for the clerk to see and note? Why rather had he not got rid of it before showing himself? Suppose it should be somebody personating Laker? In any case I determined not to be prejudiced by what I had heard of Laker's betting. A man may bet without being a thief.

'But, again, supposing it were Laker? Might he not have given his name, and displayed his wallet, and so on, while buying a ticket for France, in order to draw pursuit after himself in that direction while he made off in another, in another name, and disguised? Each supposition was plausible. And, in either case, it might happen that whoever was laying this trail would probably lay it a little farther. Charing Cross was the next point, and there I went. I already had it from Plummer that Laker had not been recognized there. Perhaps the trail had been laid in some other manner. Something left behind with Laker's name on it, perhaps? I at once thought of the umbrella with his monogram, and, making a long shot, asked for it at the lost property office, as you know. The guess was lucky: In the umbrella, as you know, I found the scrap of paper. That, I judged, had fallen in from the hand of the man carrying the umbrella. He had torn the paper in half in order to fling it away, and one piece had fallen into the loosely flapping umbrella. It is a thing that will often happen with an omnibus ticket, as you may have noticed. Also, it was proved that the umbrella was unrolled when found, and rolled immediately after. So here was a piece of paper dropped by the person who had brought the umbrella to Charing Cross and left it. I got the whole advertisement, as you remember, and I studied it. "Yob" is back-slang for "boy", and is often used in nicknames to denote a young smooth-faced thief. Gunter, the man I suspect, as a matter of fact, is known as the "Hoxton Yob". The message, then, was addressed to some one known by such a nickname. Next, "H.R. shop roast". Now, in thieves' slang, to "roast" a thing or a person is to watch it or him. They call any place a shop—notably, a thieves' den. So that this meant that some resort—perhaps the "Hoxton Row shop"—was watched. "You 1st then to-night" would be clearer, perhaps, when the rest was understood. I thought a little over the rest, and it struck me that it must be a direction to some other house, since one was warned of as being watched. Besides, there was the number, 197, and "red bl.", which would be extremely likely to mean "red blinds ", by way of clearly distinguishing the house. And then the plan of the thing was plain. You have noticed, probably, that the map of London which accompanies the Post Office Directory is divided, for convenience of reference, into numbered squares?'

'Yes. The squares are denoted by letters along the top margin and figures down the side. So that if you consult the directory, and find a place marked as being in D 5, for instance, you find vertical divisions D, and run your finger down it till it intersects horizontal division 5, and there you are.'

'Precisely. I got my Post Office Directory, and looked for "O 2". It was in North London, and took in parts of Abney Park Cemetery and Clissold Park; "2nd top" was the next sign. Very well, I counted the second street intersecting the top of the square—counting, in the usual way, from the left. That was Lordship Road. Then "3rd L". From the point where Lordship Road crossed the top of the square, I ran my finger down the road till it came to "3rd L", or, in other words, the third turning on the left—Hackworth Road. So there we were, unless my guesses were altogether wrong. "Straight mon" probably meant "straight moniker"—that is to say, the proper name, a thief's real name, in contradistinction to that he may assume. I turned over the directory till I found Hackworth Road, and found that No. 197 was inhabited by a Mr Merston. From the whole thing I judged this. There was to have been a meeting at the "H.R. shop", but that was found, at the last moment, to be watched by the police for some purpose, so that another appointment was made for this house in the suburbs. "You 1st. Then to-night"—the person addressed was to come first, and the others in the evening. They were to ask for the householder's "straight moniker"—Mr Merston. And they were to come one at a time.

'Now, then, what was this? What theory would fit it? Suppose this were a robbery, directed from afar by the advertiser. Suppose, on the day before the robbery, it was found that the place fixed for division of spoils were watched. Suppose that the principal thereupon advertised (as had already been agreed in case of emergency) in these terms. The principal in the actual robbery—the "Yob" addressed—was to go first with the booty. The others were to come after, one at a time. Anyway, the thing was good enough to follow a little further, and I determined to try No. 197 Hackworth Road. I have told you what I found there, and how it opened my eyes. I went, of course, merely on chance, to see what I might chance to see. But luck favoured, and I happened on that coat—brought back rolled up, on the evening after the robbery, doubtless by the thief who had used it, and flung carelessly into the handiest cupboard. That was this gang's mistake.'

'Well, I congratulate you,' I said. 'I hope they'll catch the rascals.'

'I rather think they will, now they know where to look. They can scarcely miss Merston, anyway. There has been very little to go upon in this case, but I stuck to the thread, however slight, and it brought me through. The rest of the case, of course, is Plummer's. It was a peculiarity of my commission that I could equally well fulfil it by catching the man with all the plunder, or by proving him innocent. Having done the latter, my work was at an end, but I left it where Plummer will be able to finish the job handsomely.'

Plummer did. Sam Gunter, Merston, and one accomplice were taken—the first and last were well known to the police—and were identified by Laker. Merston, as Hewitt had suspected, had kept the lion's share for himself, so that altogether, with what was recovered from him and the other two, nearly £11,000 was saved for Messrs Liddle, Neal & Liddle. Merston, when taken, was in the act of packing up to take a holiday abroad, and there cash his notes, which were found, neatly packed in separate thousands, in his portmanteau. As Hewitt had predicted, his gas bill was considerably less next quarter, for less than half-way through it he began a term in gaol.

As for Laker, he was reinstated, of course, with an increase of salary by way of compensation for his broken head. He had passed a terrible twenty-six hours in the cellar, unfed and unheard. Several times he had become insensible, and again and again he had thrown himself madly against the door, shouting and tearing at it, till he fell back exhausted, with broken nails and bleeding fingers. For some hours before the arrival of his rescuers he had been sitting in a sort of stupor, from which he was suddenly aroused by the sound of voices and footsteps. He was in bed for a week, and required a rest of a month in addition before he could resume his duties. Then he was quietly lectured by Mr Neal as to betting, and, I believe, dropped that practice in consequence. I am told that he is 'at the counter' now—a considerable promotion.

VI. — THE CASE OF THE LOST FOREIGNER

I have already said in more than one place that Hewitt's personal relations with the members of the London police force were of a cordial character. In the course of his work it has frequently been Hewitt's hap to learn of matters on which the police were glad of information, and that information was always passed on at once; and so long as no infringement of regulations or damage to public service were involved, Hewitt could always rely on a return in kind.

It was with a message of a useful sort that Hewitt one day dropped into Vine Street police station and asked for a particular inspector, who was not in. Hewitt sat and wrote a note, and by way of making conversation said to the inspector on duty, "Anything very startling this way to-day?"

"Nothing very startling, perhaps, as yet," the inspector replied. "But one of our chaps picked up rather an odd customer a little while ago. Lunatic of some sort, I should think—in fact, I've sent for the doctor to see him. He's a foreigner—a Frenchman, I believe. He seemed horribly weak and faint; but the oddest thing occurred when one of the men, thinking he might be hungry, brought in some bread. He went into fits of terror at the sight of it, and wouldn't be pacified till they took it away again."

"That was strange."

"Odd, wasn't it? And he was hungry too. They brought him some more a little while after, and he didn't funk it a bit,—pitched into it, in fact, like anything, and ate it all with some cold beef. It's the way with some lunatics—never the same five minutes together. He keeps crying like a baby, and saying things we can't understand. As it happens, there's nobody in just now who speaks French."

"I speak French," Hewitt replied. "Shall I try him?"

"Certainly, if you will. He's in the men's room below. They've been making him as comfortable as possible by the fire until the doctor comes. He's a long time. I expect he's got a case on."

Hewitt found his way to the large mess-room, where three or four policemen in their shirt-sleeves were curiously regarding a young man of very disordered appearance who sat on a chair by the fire. He was pale, and exhibited marks of bruises on his face, while over one eye was a scarcely healed cut. His figure was small and slight, his coat was torn, and he sat with a certain indefinite air of shivering suffering. He started and looked round apprehensively as Hewitt entered. Hewitt bowed smilingly, wished him good-day, speaking in French, and asked him if he spoke the language.

The man looked up with a dull expression, and after an effort or two, as of one who stutters, burst out with, "Je le nie!"

"That's strange," Hewitt observed to the men. "I ask him if he speaks French, and he says he denies it—speaking in French."

"He's been saying that very often, sir," one of the men answered, "as well as other things we can't make anything of."

Hewitt placed his hand kindly on the man's shoulder and asked his name. The reply was for a little while an inarticulate gurgle, presently merging into a meaningless medley of words and syllables—"Qu'est ce qu'—il n'a—Leystar Squarr—sacré nom—not spik it—quel chemin—sank you ver' mosh—je le nie! je le nie!" He paused, stared, and then, as though realizing his helplessness, he burst into tears.

"He's been a-cryin' two or three times," said the man who had spoken before. "He was a-cryin' when we found him."

Several more attempts Hewitt made to communicate with the man, but though he seemed to comprehend what was meant, he replied with nothing but meaningless gibber, and finally gave up the attempt, and, leaning against the side of the fireplace, buried his head in the bend of his arm.

Then the doctor arrived and made his examination. While it was in progress Hewitt took aside the policeman who had been speaking before and questioned him further. He had himself found the Frenchman in a dull back street by Golden Square, where the man was standing helpless and trembling, apparently quite bewildered and very weak. He had brought him in, without having been able to learn anything about him. One or two shopkeepers in the street where he was found were asked, but knew nothing of him—indeed, had never seen him before.

"But the curiousest thing," the policeman proceeded, "was in this 'ere room, when I brought him a loaf to give him a bit of a snack, seein' he looked so weak an' 'ungry. You'd 'a thought we was a-goin' to poison 'im. He fair screamed at the very sight o' the bread, an' he scrouged hisself up in that corner an' put his hands in front of his face. I couldn't make out what was up at first—didn't tumble to it's bein' the bread he was frightened of, seein' as he looked like a man as 'ud be frightened at anything else afore that. But the nearer I came with it the more he yelled, so I took it away an' left it outside, an' then he calmed down. An' s'elp me, when I cut some bits off that there very loaf an' brought 'em in, with a bit o' beef, he just went for 'em like one o'clock. He wasn't frightened o' no bread then, you bet. Rum thing, how the fancies takes 'em when they're a bit touched, ain't it? All one way one minute, all the other the next."

"Yes, it is. By the way, have you another uncut loaf in the place?"

"Yes, sir. Half a dozen if you like."

"One will be enough. I am going over to speak to the doctor. Wait awhile until he seems very quiet and fairly comfortable; then bring a loaf in quietly and put it on the table, not far from his elbow. Don't attract his attention to what you are doing."

The doctor stood looking thoughtfully down on the Frenchman, who, for his part, stared gloomily, but tranquilly, at the fire-place. Hewitt stepped quietly over to the doctor and, without disturbing the man by the fire, said interrogatively, "Aphasia?"

The doctor tightened his lips, frowned, and nodded significantly. "Motor," he murmured, just loudly enough for Hewitt to hear; "and there's a general nervous break-down as well, I should say. By the way, perhaps there's no agraphia. Have you tried him with pen and paper?"

Pen and paper were brought and set before the man. He was told, slowly and distinctly, that he was among friends, whose only object was to restore him to his proper health. Would he write his name and address, and any other information he might care to give about himself, on the paper before him?

The Frenchman took the pen and stared at the paper; then slowly, and with much hesitation, he traced these marks:—

The man paused after the last of these futile characters, and his pen stabbed into the paper with a blot, as he dazedly regarded his work. Then with a groan he dropped it, and his face sank again into the bend of his arm.

The doctor took the paper and handed it to Hewitt. "Complete agraphia, you see," he said. "He can't write a word. He begins to write 'Monsieur' from sheer habit in beginning letters thus; but the word tails off into a scrawl. Then his attempts become mere scribble, with just a trace of some familiar word here and there—but quite meaningless all."

Although he had never before chanced to come across a case of aphasia (happily a rare disease), Hewitt was acquainted with its general nature. He knew that it might arise either from some physical injury to the brain, or from a break-down consequent on some terrible nervous strain. He knew that in the case of motor aphasia the sufferer, though fully conscious of all that goes on about him, and though quite understanding what is said to him is entirely powerless to put his own thoughts into spoken words—has lost, in fact, the connection between words and their spoken symbols. Also that in most bad cases agraphia—the loss of ability to write words with any reference to their meaning—is commonly an accompaniment.

"You will have him taken to the infirmary, I suppose?" Hewitt asked.

"Yes," the doctor replied. "I shall go and see about it at once."

The man looked up again as they spoke. The policeman had, in accordance with Hewitt's request, placed a loaf of bread on the table near him, and now as he looked up he caught sight of it. He started visibly and paled, but gave no such signs of abject terror as the policeman had previously observed. He appeared nervous and uneasy, however, and presently reached stealthily toward the loaf. Hewitt continued to talk to the doctor, while closely watching the Frenchman's behaviour from the corner of his eye.

The loaf was what is called a "plain cottage," of solid and regular shape. The man reached it and immediately turned it bottom up on the table. Then he sank back in his chair with a more contented expression, though his gaze was still directed toward the loaf. The policeman grinned silently at this curious manoeuvre.

The doctor left, and Hewitt accompanied him to the door of the room. "He will not be moved just yet, I take it?" Hewitt asked as they parted.

"It may take an hour or two," the doctor replied. "Are you anxious to keep him here?"

"Not for long; but I think there's a curious inside to the case, and I may perhaps learn something of it by a little watching. But I can't spare very long."

At a sign from Hewitt the loaf was removed.

Then Hewitt pulled the small table closer to the Frenchman and pushed the pen and sheets of paper toward him. The manoeuvre had its result. The man looked up and down the room vacantly once or twice and then began to turn the papers over.

From that he went to dipping the pen in the inkpot, and presently he was scribbling at random on the loose sheets. Hewitt affected to leave him entirely alone, and seemed to be absorbed in a contemplation of a photograph of a police-division brass band that hung on the wall, but he saw every scratch the man made.

At first there was nothing but meaningless scrawls and attempted words. Then rough sketches appeared, of a man's head, a chair or what not. On the mantelpiece stood a small clock—apparently a sort of humble presentation piece, the body of the clock being set in a horse-shoe frame, with crossed whips behind it. After a time the Frenchman's eyes fell on this, and he began a crude sketch of it. That he relinquished, and went on with other random sketches and scribblings on the same piece of paper, sketching and scribbling over the sketches in a half mechanical sort of way, as of one who trifles with a pen during a brown study. Beginning at the top left-hand corner of the paper, he travelled all round it till he arrived at the left-hand bottom corner. Then dashing his pen hastily across his last sketch he dropped it, and with a great shudder turned away again and hid his face by the fireplace.

Hewitt turned at once and seized the papers on the table. He stuffed them all into his coat-pocket, with the exception of the last which the man had been engaged on, and this, a facsimile of which is subjoined, he studied earnestly for several minutes.

Hewitt wished the men good-day, and made his way to the inspector.

"Well," the inspector said, "not much to be got out of him, is there? The doctor will be sending for him presently."

"I fancy," said Hewitt, "that this may turn out a very important case. Possibly—quite possibly—I may not have guessed correctly, and so I won't tell you anything of it till I know a little more. But what I want now is a messenger. Can I send somebody at once in a cab to my friend Brett at his chambers?"

"Certainly. I'll find somebody. Want to write a note?"

Hewitt wrote and despatched a note, which reached me in less than ten minutes. Then he asked the inspector, "Have you searched the Frenchman?"

"Oh, yes. We went all over him, when we found he couldn't explain himself, to see if we could trace his friends or his address. He didn't seem to mind. But there wasn't a single thing in his pocket—not a single thing, barring a rag of a pocket-handkerchief with no marking on it."

"You noticed that somebody had stolen his watch, I suppose?"

"Well, he hadn't got one."

"But he had one of those little vertical buttonholes in his waistcoat, used to fasten a watchguard to, and it was much worn and frayed, so that he must be in the habit of carrying a watch; and it is gone."

"Yes, and everything else too, eh? Looks like robbery. He's had a knock or two in the face—notice that?"

"I saw the bruises and the cut, of course; and his collar has been broken away, with the back button; somebody has taken him by the collar or throat. Was he wearing a hat when he was found?"

"No."

"That would imply that he had only just left a house. What street was he found in?"

"Henry Street—a little off Golden Square. Low street, you know."

"Did the constable notice a door open near by?"

The inspector shook his head. "Half the doors in the street are open," he said, "pretty nearly all day."

"Ah, then there's nothing in that. I don't think he lives there, by the bye. I fancy he comes from more in the Seven Dials or Drury Lane direction. Did you notice anything about the man that gave you a clue to his occupation—or at any rate to his habits?"

"Can't say I did."

"Well, just take a look at the back of his coat before he goes away—just over the loins. Good-day."

As I have said, Hewitt's messenger was quick. I happened to be in—having lately returned from a latish lunch—when he arrived with this note:—

"My dear B.,—I meant to have lunched with you to-day, but have been kept. I expect you are idle this afternoon, and I have a case that will interest you—perhaps be useful to you from a journalistic point of view. If you care to see anything of it, cab away at once to Fitzroy Square, south side, where I'll meet you. I will wait no later than 3.30. Yours, M. H."

I had scarce a quarter of an hour, so I seized my hat and left my chambers at once. As it happened, my cab and Hewitt's burst into Fitzroy Square from opposite sides almost at the same moment, so that we lost no time.

"Come," said Hewitt, taking my arm and marching me out, "we are going to look for some stabling. Try to feel as though you'd just set up a brougham and had come out to look for a place to put it in. I fear we may have to delude some person with that belief presently."

"Why—what do you want stables for? And why make me your excuse?"

"As to what I want the stables for—really I'm not altogether sure myself. As to making you an excuse—well, even the humblest excuse is better than none. But come, here are some stables. Not good enough, though, even if any of them were empty. Come on."

We had stopped for an instant at the entrance to a small alley of rather dirty stables, and Hewitt, paying apparently but small attention to the stables themselves, had looked sharply about him with his gaze in the air.

"I know this part of London pretty well," Hewitt observed, "and I can only remember one other range of stabling near by; we must try that. As a matter of fact, I'm coming here on little more than conjecture, though I shall be surprised if there isn't something in it. Do you know anything of aphasia?"

"I have heard of it, of course, though I can't say I remember ever knowing a case."

"I've seen one to-day—very curious case. The man's a Frenchman, discovered helpless in the street by a policeman. The only thing he can say that has any meaning in it at all is 'je le nie,' and that he says mechanically, without in the least knowing what he is saying. And he can't write. But he got sketching and scrawling various things on some paper, and his scrawls—together with another thing or two—have given me an idea. We're following it up now. When we are less busy, and in a quiet place, I'll show you the sketches and explain things generally; there's no time now, and I may want your help for a bit, in which case ignorance may prevent you spoiling things, you clumsy ruffian. Hullo! here we are, I think!"

We had stopped at the end of another stableyard, rather dirtier than the first. The stables were sound but inelegant sheds, and one or two appeared to be devoted to other purposes, having low chimneys, on one of which an old basket was rakishly set by way of cowl. Beside the entrance a worn-out old board was nailed, with the legend, "Stabling to Let," in letters formerly white on a ground formerly black.

"Come," said Hewitt, "we'll explore."

We picked our way over the greasy cobble-stones and looked about us. On the left was the wall enclosing certain back-yards, and on the right the stables. Two doors in the middle of these were open, and a butcher's young man, who with his shiny bullet head would have been known for a butcher's young man anywhere, was wiping over the new-washed wheel of a smart butcher's cart.

"Good-day," Hewitt said pleasantly to the young man. "I notice there's some stabling to let here. Now, where should I inquire about it?"

"Jones, Whitfield Street," the young man answered, giving the wheel a final spin. "But there's only one little place to let now, I think, and it ain't very grand."

"Oh, which is that?"

"Next but one to the street there. A chap 'ad it for wood-choppin', but 'e chucked it. There ain't room for more'n a donkey an' a barrow."

"Ah, that's a pity. We're not particular, but want something big enough, and we don't mind paying a fair price. Perhaps we might make an arrangement with somebody here who has a stable?"

The young man shook his head.

"I shouldn't think so," he said doubtfully; "they're mostly shop-people as wants all the room theirselves. My guv'nor couldn't do nothink, I know. These 'ere two stables ain't scarcely enough for all 'e wants as it is. Then there's Barkett the greengrocer 'ere next door. That ain't no good. Then, next to that, there's the little place as is to let, and at the end there's Griffith's at the buttershop."

"And those the other way?"

"Well, this 'ere first one's Curtis's, Euston Road—that's a butter-shop, too, an' 'e 'as the next after that. The last one, up at the end—I dunno quite whose that is. It ain't been long took, but I b'lieve it's some foreign baker's. I ain't ever see anythink come out of it, though; but there's a 'orse there, I know—I seen the feed took in."

Hewitt turned thoughtfully away.

"Thanks," he said. "I suppose we can't manage it, then. Good-day."

We walked to the street as the butcher's young man wheeled in his cart and flung away his pail of water.

"Will you just hang about here, Brett," he asked, "while I hurry round to the nearest ironmonger's? I shan't be gone long. We're going to work a little burglary. Take note if anybody comes to that stable at the farther end."

He hurried away and I waited. In a few moments the butcher's young man shut his doors and went whistling down the street, and in a few moments more Hewitt appeared.

"Come," he said, "there's nobody about now; we'll lose no time. I've bought a pair of pliers and a few nails."

We re-entered the yard at the door of the last stable. Hewitt stooped and examined the padlock. Taking a nail in his pliers he bent it carefully against the brick wall. Then using the nail as a key, still held by the pliers, and working the padlock gently in his left hand, in an astonishingly few seconds he had released the hasp and taken off the padlock. "I'm not altogether a bad burglar," he remarked. "Not so bad, really."

The padlock fastened a bar which, when removed, allowed the door to be opened. Opening it, Hewitt immediately seized a candle stuck in a bottle which stood on a shelf, pulled me in, and closed the door behind us.

"We'll do this by candle-light," he said, as he struck a match. "If the door were left open it would be seen from the street. Keep your ears open in case anybody comes down the yard."

The part of the shed that we stood in was used as a coach-house, and was occupied by a rather shabby tradesman's cart, the shafts of which rested on the ground. From the stall adjoining came the sound of the shuffling and trampling of an impatient horse.

We turned to the cart. On the name-board at the side were painted in worn letters the words, "Schuyler, Baker." The address, which had been below, was painted out.

Hewitt took out the pins and let down the tailboard. Within the cart was a new bed-mattress which covered the whole surface at the bottom. I felt it, pressed it from the top, and saw that it was an ordinary spring mattress—perhaps rather unusually soft in the springs. It seemed a curious thing to keep in a baker's cart.

Hewitt, who had set the candle on a convenient shelf, plunged his arm into the farthermost recesses of the cart and brought forth a very long French loaf, and then another. Diving again he produced certain loaves of the sort known as the "plain cottage "—two sets of four each, each set baked together in a row. "Feel this bread," said Hewitt, and I felt it. It was stale—almost as hard as wood.

Hewitt produced a large pocket-knife, and with what seemed to me to be superfluous care and elaboration, cut into the top of one of the cottage loaves. Then he inserted his fingers in the gap he had made and firmly but slowly tore the hard bread into two pieces. He pulled away the crumb from within till there was nothing left but a rather thick outer shell.

"No," he said, rather to himself than to me, "there's nothing in that." He lifted one of the very long French loaves and measured it against the interior of the cart. It had before been propped diagonally, and now it was noticeable that it was just a shade longer than the inside of the cart was wide. Jammed in, in fact, it held firmly. Hewitt produced his knife again, and divided this long loaf in the centre; there was nothing but bread in that. The horse in the stall fidgeted more than ever.

"That horse hasn't been fed lately, I fancy," Hewitt said. "We'll give the poor chap a bit of this hay in the corner."

"But," I said, "what about this bread? What did you expect to find in it? I can't see what you're driving at."

"I'll tell you," Hewitt replied, "I'm driving after something I expect to find; and close at hand here, too. How are your nerves to-day—pretty steady? The thing may try them."

Before I could reply there was a sound of footsteps in the yard outside, approaching. Hewitt lifted his finger instantly for silence and whispered hurriedly, "There's only one. If he comes here, we grab him."

The steps came nearer and stopped outside the door. There was a pause, and then a slight drawing in of breath, as of a person suddenly surprised. At that moment the door was slightly shifted ajar and an eye peeped in.

"Catch him!" said Hewitt aloud, as we sprang to the door. "He mustn't get away!"

I had been nearer the doorway, and was first through it. The stranger ran down the yard at his best, but my legs were the longer, and half-way to the street I caught him by the shoulder and swung him round. Like lightning he whipped out a knife, and I flung in my left instantly on the chance of flooring him. It barely checked him, however, and the knife swung short of my chest by no more than two inches; but Hewitt had him by the wrist and tripped him forward on his face. He struggled like a wild beast, and Hewitt had to stand on his forearm and force up his wrist till the bones were near breaking before he dropped his knife. But throughout the struggle the man never shouted, called for help, nor, indeed, made the slightest sound, and we on our part were equally silent.

It was quickly over, of course, for he was on his face, and we were two. We dragged our prisoner into the stable and closed the door behind us. So far as we had seen, nobody had witnessed the capture from the street, though, of course, we had been too busy to be certain.

"There's a set of harness hanging over at the back," said Hewitt; "I think we'll tie him up with the traces and reins—nothing like leather. We don't need a gag; I know he won't shout."

While I got the straps Hewitt held the prisoner by a peculiar neck-and-wrist grip that forbade him to move except at the peril of a snapped arm. He had probably never been a person of pleasant aspect, being short, strongly and squatly built, large and ugly of feature, and wild and dirty of hair and beard. And now, his face flushed with struggling and smeared with mud from the stableyard, his nose bleeding and his forehead exhibiting a growing bump, he looked particularly repellent. We strapped his elbows together behind, and as he sullenly ignored a demand for the contents of his pockets Hewitt unceremoniously turned them out. Helpless as he was, the man struggled to prevent this, though, of course, ineffectually. There were papers, tobacco, a bunch of keys, and various odds and ends. Hewitt was glancing hastily at the papers when, suddenly dropping them, he caught the prisoner by the shoulder and pulled him away from a partly-consumed hay-truss which stood in a corner, and toward which he had quietly sidled.

"Keep him still," said Hewitt; "we haven't examined this place yet." And he commenced to pull away the hay from the corner.

Presently a large piece of sackcloth was revealed, and this being lifted left visible below it another batch of loaves of the same sort as we had seen in the cart. There were a dozen of them in one square batch, and the only thing about them that differed them from those in the cart was their position, for the batch lay bottom side up.

"That's enough, I think," Hewitt said. "Don't touch them, for Heaven's sake!" He picked up the papers he had dropped. "That has saved us a little search," he continued. "See here, Brett; I was in the act of telling you my suspicions when this little affair interrupted me. If you care to look at one or two of these letters you'll see what I should have told you. It's Anarchism and bombs, of course. I'm about as certain as I can be that there's a reversible dynamite bomb inside each of those innocent loaves, though I assure you I don't mean meddling with them now. But see here. Will you go and bring in a four-wheeler? Bring it right down the yard. There's more to do, and we mustn't attract attention."

I hurried away and found the cab. The meaning of the loaves, the cart, and the spring-mattress was now plain. There was an Anarchist plot to carry out a number of explosions probably simul' taneously, in different parts of the city. I had, of course, heard much of the terrible "reversing" bombs—those bombs which, containing a tube of acid plugged by wadding, required no fuse, and only needed to be inverted to be set going to explode in a few minutes. The loaves containing these bombs would form an effectual "blind," and they were to be distributed, probably in broad daylight, in the most natural manner possible, in a baker's cart. A man would be waiting near the scene of each contemplated explosion. He would be given a loaf taken from the inverted batch. He would take it—perhaps wrapped in paper, but still inverted, and apparently the most innocent object possible—to the spot selected, deposit it, right side up—which would reverse the inner tube and set up the action—in some quiet corner, behind a door or what not, and make his own escape, while the explosion tore down walls and—if the experiment were lucky—scattered the flesh and bones of unsuspecting people.

The infernal loaves were made and kept reversed, to begin with, in order to stand more firmly, and—if observed—more naturally, when turned over to explode. Even if a child picked up the loaf and carried it off, that child at least would be blown to atoms, which at any rate would have been something for the conspirators to congratulate themselves upon. The spring-mattress, of course, was to ease the jolting to the bombs, and obviate any random jerking loose of the acid, which might have had the deplorable result of sacrificing the valuable life of the conspirator who drove the cart. The other loaves, too, with no explosive contents, had their use. The two long ones, which fitted across the inside of the cart, would be jammed across so as to hold the bombs in the centre, and the others would be used to pack the batch on the other sides and prevent any dangerous slipping about. The thing seemed pretty plain, except that as yet I had no idea of how Hewitt learned anything of the business.

I brought the four-wheeler up to the door of the stable and we thrust the man into it, and Hewitt locked the stable door with its proper key. Then we drove off to Tottenham Court Road police-station, and, by Hewitt's order, straight into the yard.

In less than ten minutes from our departure from the stable our prisoner was finally secured, and Hewitt was deep in consultation with police officials. Messengers were sent and telegrams despatched, and presently Hewitt came to me with information.

"The name of the helpless Frenchman the police found this morning," he said, "appears to be Gérard—at least I am almost certain of it. Among the papers found on the prisoner—whose full name doesn't appear, but who seems to be spoken of as Luigi (he is Italian)—among the papers, I say, is a sort of notice convening a meeting for this evening to decide as to the 'final punishment' to be awarded the 'traitor Gérard, now in charge of comrade Pingard.'

"The place of meeting is not mentioned, but it seems more than probable that it will be at the Bakunin Club, not five minutes' walk from this place. The police have all these places under quiet observation, of course, and that is the club at which apparently important Anarchist meetings have been held lately. It is the only club that has never been raided as yet, and, it would seem, the only one they would feel at all safe in using for anything important.

"Moreover, Luigi just now simply declined to open his mouth when asked where the meeting was to be, and said nothing when the names of several other places were suggested, but suddenly found his tongue at the mention of the Bakunin Club, and denied vehemently that the meeting was to be there—it was the only thing he uttered. So that it seems pretty safe to assume that it is to be there. Now, of course, the matter's very serious. Men have been despatched to take charge of the stable very quietly, and the club is to be taken possession of at once—also very quietly. It must be done without a moment's delay, and as there is a chance that the only detective officers within reach at the moment may be known by sight, I have undertaken to get in first. Perhaps you'll come? We may have to take the door with a rush."

Of course I meant to miss nothing if I could help it, and said so.

"Very well," replied Hewitt, "we'll get ourselves up a bit." He began taking off his collar and tie. "It is getting dusk," he proceeded, "and we shan't want old clothes to make ourselves look sufficiently shabby. We're both wearing bowler hats, which is lucky. Make a dent in yours—if you can do so without permanently damaging it."

We got rid of our collars and made chokers of our ties. We turned our coat-collars up at one side only, and then, with dented hats worn raffishly, and our hands in our pockets, we looked disreputable enough for all practical purposes in twilight. A cordon of plain-clothes police had already been forming round the club, we were told, and so we sallied forth. We turned into Windmill Street, crossed Whitfield

Street, and in a turning or two we came to the Bakunin Club. I could see no sign of anything like a ring of policemen, and said so. Hewitt chuckled. "Of course not," he said; "they don't go about a job of this sort with drums beating and flags flying. But they are all there, and some are watching us. There is the house. I'll negotiate."

The house was one of the very shabby passé sort that abound in that quarter. The very narrow area was railed over, and almost choked with rubbish. Visible above it were three floors, the lowest indicated by the door and one window, and the other two by two windows each—mean and dirty all. A faint light appeared in the top floor, and another from somewhere behind the refuse-heaped area. Everywhere else was in darkness. Hewitt looked intently into the area, but it was impossible to discern anything behind the sole grimy patch of window that was visible. Then we stepped lightly up the three or four steps to the door and rang the bell.

We could hear slippered feet mounting a stair and approaching. A latch was shifted, a door opened six inches, an indistinct face appeared, and a female voice asked, "Qui est là?"

"Deux camarades," Hewitt grunted testily. "Ouvrez vite."

I had noticed that the door was kept from opening further by a short chain. This chain the woman unhooked from the door, but still kept the latter merely ajar, as though intending to assure herself still further. But Hewitt immediately pushed the door back, planted his foot against it, and entered, asking carelessly as he did so, "Où se trouve Luigi?"

I followed on his heels, and in the dark could just distinguish that Hewitt pushed the woman instantly against the wall and clapped his hand to her mouth. At the same moment a file of quiet men were suddenly visible ascending the steps at my heels. They were the police.

The door was closed behind us almost noiselessly, and a match was struck. Two men stood at the bottom of the stairs, and the others searched the house. Only two men were found—both in a top room. They were secured and brought down.

The woman was now ungagged, and she used her tongue at a great rate. One of the men was a small, meek-looking slip of a fellow, and he appeared to be the woman's husband. "Eh, messieurs le police," she exclaimed vehemently, "it ees not of 'im, mon pauvre Pierre, zat you sail rrun in. 'Im and me—we are not of the clob—we work only—we housekeep."

Hewitt whispered to an officer, and the two men were taken below. Then Hewitt spoke to the woman, whose protests had not ceased. "You say you are not of the club," he said, "but what is there to prove that? If you are but housekeepers, as you say, you have nothing to fear. But you can only prove it by giving the police information. For instance, now, about Gérard. What have they done with him?"

"Jean Pingard—'im you 'ave take downstairs—'e 'ave lose 'im. Jean Pingard get last night all a-boosa—all dronk like zis "—she rolled her head and shoulders to express intoxication—"and he sleep too much to-day, when Émile go out, and Gérard, he go too, and nobody know. I will tell you anysing. We are not of the clob—we housekeep, me and Pierre."

"But what did they do to Gérard before he went away?"

The woman was ready and anxious to tell anything. Gérard had been selected to do something—what it was exactly she did not know, but there was a horse and cart, and he was to drive it. Where the horse and cart was also she did not know, but Gérard had driven a cart before in his work for a baker, and he was to drive one in connection with some scheme among the members of the club. But le pauvre Gérard at the last minute disliked to drive the cart; he had fear. He did not say he had fear, but he prepared a letter—a letter that was not signed. The letter was to be sent to the police, and it told them the whereabouts of the horse and cart, so that the police might seize these things, and then there would be nothing for Gérard, who had fear, to do in the way of driving. No, he did not betray the names of the comrades, but he told the place of the horse and the cart.

Nevertheless, the letter was never sent. There was suspicion, and the letter was found in a pocket and read. Then there was a meeting, and Gérard was confronted with his letter. He could say nothing but "Je le nie!"—found no explanation but that. There was much noise, and she had observed from a staircase, from which one might see through a ventilating hole, Gérard had much fear—very much fear. His face was white, and it moved; he prayed for mercy, and they talked of killing him. It was discussed how he should be killed, and the poor Gérard was more terrified. He was made to take off his collar, and a razor was drawn across his throat, though without cutting him, till he fainted.

Then water was flung over him, and he was struck in the face till he revived. He again repeated, "je le nie! je le nie!" and nothing more. Then one struck him with a bottle, and another with a stick; the point of a knife was put against his throat and held there, but this time he did not faint, but cried softly, as a man who is drunk, "je le nie! je le nie!" So they tied a handkerchief about his neck, and twisted it till his face grew purple and black, and his eyes were round and terrible, and then they struck his face, and he fainted again. But they took away the handkerchief, having fear that they could not easily get rid of the body if he were killed, for there was no preparation. So they decided to meet again and discuss when there would be preparation. Wherefore they took him away to the rooms of Jean Pingard—of Jean and Émile Pingard—in Henry Street, Golden Square. But Émile Pingard had gone out, and Jean was drunk and slept, and they lost him. Jean Pingard was he downstairs—the taller of the two; the other was but le pauvre Pierre, who, with herself, was not of the club. They worked only; they were the keepers of the house. There was nothing for which they should be arrested, and she would give the police any information they might ask.

"As I thought, you see," Hewitt said to me, "the man's nerves have broken down under the terror and the strain, and aphasia is the result. I think I told you that the only articulate thing he could say was 'Je le nie!' and now we know how those words were impressed on him till he now pronounces them mechanically, with no idea of their meaning. Come, we can do no more here now. But wait a moment."

There were footsteps outside. The light was removed, and a policeman went to the door and opened it as soon as the bell rang. Three men stepped in one after another, and the door was immediately shut behind them—they were prisoners.

We left quietly, and although we, of course, expected it, it was not till the next morning that we learned absolutely that the largest arrest of Anarchists ever made in this country was made at the Bakunin Club that night. Each man as he came was admitted—and collared.

We made our way to Luzatti's, and it was over our dinner that Hewitt put me in full possession of the earlier facts of this case, which I have set down as impersonal narrative in their proper place at the beginning.

"But," I said, "what of that aimless scribble you spoke of that Gérard made in the police station? Can I see it?"

Hewitt turned to where his coat hung behind him and took a handful of papers from his pocket.

"Most of these," he said, "mean nothing at all. That is what he wrote at first," and he handed me the first of the two papers which were presented in facsimile in the earlier part of this narrative.

"You see," he said, "he has begun mechanically from long use to write 'monsieur'—the usual beginning of a letter. But he scarcely makes three letters before tailing off into sheer scribble. He tries again and again, and although once there is something very like 'que,' and once something like a word preceded by a negative 'n,' the whole thing is meaningless.

"This," (he handed me the other paper which has been printed in facsimile) "does mean something, though Gérard never intended it. Can you spot the meaning? Really, I think it's pretty plain—especially now that you know as much as I about the day's adventures. The thing at the top left-hand corner, I may tell you, Gérard intended for a sketch of a clock on the mantelpiece in the police station."

I stared hard at the paper, but could make nothing whatever of it. "I only see the horse-shoe clock," I said, "and a sort of second, unsuccessful attempt to draw it again. Then there is a horseshoe dotted, but scribbled over, and then a sort of kite or balloon on a string, a Highlander, and—well, I don't understand it, I confess. Tell me."

"I'll explain what I learned from that," Hewitt said, "and also what led me to look for it. From what the inspector told me, I judged the man to be in a very curious state, and I took a fancy to see him. Most I was curious to know why he should have a terror of bread at one moment and eat it ravenously at another. When I saw him I felt pretty sure that he was not mad, in the common sense of the term. As far as I could judge it seemed to be a case of aphasia.

"Then when the doctor came I had a chat (as I have already told you) with the policeman who found the man. He told me about the incident of the bread with rather more detail than I had had from the inspector. Thus it was plain that the man was terrified at the bread only when it was in the form of a loaf, and ate it eagerly when it was cut into pieces. That was one thing to bear in mind. He was not afraid of bread, but only of a loaf.

"Very well. I asked the policeman to find another uncut loaf, and to put it near the man when his attention was diverted. Meantime the doctor reported that my suspicion as to aphasia was right. The man grew more comfortable, and was assured that he was among friends and had nothing to fear, so that when at length he found the loaf near his elbow he was not so violently terrified, only very uneasy. I watched him and saw him turn it bottom up—a very curious thing to do; he immediately became less uneasy—the turning over of the loaf seemed to have set his mind at, rest in some way. This was more curious still. I thought for some little while before accepting the bomb theory as the most probable.

"The doctor left, and I determined to give the man another chance with pen and paper. I felt pretty certain that if he were allowed to scribble and sketch as he pleased, sooner or later he would do something that would give me some sort of a hint. I left him entirely alone and let him do as he pleased, but I watched.

"After all the futile scribble which you have seen, he began to sketch, first a man's head, then a chair— just what he might happen to see in the room. Presently he took to the piece of paper you have before you. He observed that clock and began to sketch it, then went on to other things, such as you see, scribbling idly over most of them when finished. When he had made the last of the sketches he made a hasty scrawl of his pen over it and broke down. It had brought his terror to his mind again somehow.

"I seized the paper and examined it closely. Now just see. Ignore the clock, which was merely a sketch of a thing before him, and look at the three things following. What are they? A horseshoe, a captive balloon, and a Highlander. Now, can't you think of something those three things in that order suggest?"

I could think of nothing whatever, and I confessed as much.

"Think, now. Tottenham Court Road!"

I started. "Of course," I said. "That never struck me. There's the Horse-shoe Hotel, with the sign outside, there's the large toy and fancy shop half-way up, where they have a captive balloon moored to the roof as an advertisement, and there's the tobacco and snuff shop on the left, toward the other end, where they have a life-size wooden Highlander at the door—an uncommon thing, indeed, nowadays."

"You are right. The curious conjunction struck me at once. There they are, all three, and just in the order in which one meets them going up from Oxford Street. Also, as if to confirm the conjecture, note the dotted horse-shoe. Don't you remember that at night the Horse-shoe Hotel sign is illuminated by two rows of gas lights?

"Now here was my clue at last. Plainly, this man, in his mechanical sketching, was following a regular train of thought, and unconsciously illustrating it as he went along. Many people in perfect health and mental soundness do the same thing if a pen and a piece of waste paper be near. The man's train of thought led him, in memory, up Tottenham Court Road, and further, to where some disagreeable recollection upset him. It was my business to trace this train of thought. Do you remember the feat of Dupin in Poe's story, 'The Murders in the Rue Morgue'—how he walks by his friend's side in silence for some distance, and then suddenly breaks out with a divination of his thoughts, having silently traced them from a fruiterer with a basket, through paving-stones, Epicurus, Dr. Nichols, the constellation Orion, and a Latin poem, to a cobbler lately turned actor?

"Well, it was some such task as this (but infinitely simpler, as a matter of fact) that was set me. This man begins by drawing the horse-shoe clock. Having done with that, and with the horse-shoe still in his mind, he starts to draw a horse-shoe simply. It is a failure, and he scribbles it out. His mind at once turns to the Horse-shoe Hotel, which he knows from frequently passing it, and its sign of gas-jets. He sketches that, making dots for the gas lights. Once started in Tottenham Court Road, his mind naturally follows his usual route along it. He remembers the advertising captive balloon halfway up, and down that goes on his paper. In imagination he crosses the road, and keeps on till he comes to the very noticeable Highlander outside the tobacconist's. That is sketched. Thus it is plain that a familiar route with him was from New Oxford Street up Tottenham Court Road.

"At the police-station I ventured to guess from this that he lived somewhere near Seven Dials. Perhaps before long we shall know if this was right. But to return to the sketches. After the Highlander there is something at first not very distinct. A little examination, however, shows it to be intended for a chimney-pot partly covered with a basket. Now an old basket, stuck sideways on a chimney by way of cowl, is not an uncommon thing in parts of the country, but it is very unusual in London. Probably, then, it would be in some bystreet or alley. Next and last, there is a horse's head, and it was at this that the man's trouble returned to him.

"Now, when one goes to a place and finds a horse there, that place is not uncommonly a stable; and, as a matter of fact, the basket-cowl would be much more likely to be found in use in a range of back stabling than anywhere else. Suppose, then, that after taking the direction indicated in the sketches— the direction of Fitzroy Square, in fact—one were to find a range of stabling with a basket-cowl visible about it? I know my London pretty well, as you are aware, and I could remember but two likely stable-yards in that particular part—the two we looked at, in the second of which you may possibly have noticed just such a basket-cowl as I have been speaking of.

"Well, what we did you know, and that we found confirmation of my conjecture about the loaves you also know. It was the recollection of the horse and cart, and what they were to transport, and what the end of it all had been, that upset Gérard as he drew the horse's head. You will notice that the sketches have not been done in separate rows, left to right—they have simply followed one another all round the paper, which means preoccupation and unconsciousness on the part of the man who made them."

"But," I asked, "supposing those loaves to contain bombs, how were the bombs put there? Baking the bread round them would have been risky, wouldn't it?"

"Certainly. What they did was to cut the loaves, each row, down the centre. Then most of the crumb was scooped out, the explosive inserted, and the sides joined up and glued. I thought you had spotted the joins, though they certainly were neat."

"No, I didn't examine closely. Luigi, of course, had been told off for a daily visit to feed the horse, and that is how we caught him."

"One supposes so. They hadn't rearranged their plans as to going on with the outrages after Gérard's defection. By the way, I noticed that he was accustomed to driving when I first saw him. There was an unmistakable mark on his coat, just at the small of the back, that drivers get who lean against a rail in a cart."

The loaves were examined by official experts, and, as everybody now knows, were found to contain, as Hewitt had supposed, large charges of dynamite. What became of some half-dozen of the men captured is also well known: their sentences were exemplary.

ARTHUR MORRISON - A CONCISE BIBLIOGRAPHY

Tales of Mean Streets (1894)
Martin Hewitt, Investigator (1894)
Zig-Zags At The Zoo (1894)
The Chronicles of Martin Hewitt (1895)
The Adventures of Martin Hewitt (1896)
A Child of the Jago (1896)

The Dorrington Deed Box (1897)
To London Town (1899)
Cunning Murrell (1900)
The Hole in the Wall (1902)
The Red Triangle (1903)
The Green Eye of Goona (Released in the US as The Green Diamond) (1904)
Divers Vanities (1905)
Green Ginger (1909)
Fiddle O'Dreams And More (1933)

www.ingramcontent.com/pod-product-compliance
Lightning Source LLC
Chambersburg PA
CBHW071410170626
46811CB00003B/1338